Words of Gold

CHERYL BUENGER

Like apples of gold in settings of silver
is a word spoken at the right time.

Proverbs 25:11

WORDS OF GOLD
Copyright © 2016 by Cheryl Buenger

Printed in the United States of America.

This book is a work of fiction. Names, characters, businesses,
organizations, places, events and incidents either are the
product of the author's imagination or are used fictitiously. Any
resemblance to actual persons, living or dead, events, or locales
is entirely coincidental.

For contact information visit:
http://www.wordsofgold.me

Cover design by Gretchen Herrmann, Primary Colors
Editing by Ashley Buenger, ashley.buenger@gmail.com
Available on Kindle and online stores
First Edition: December 2016
All rights reserved.
ISBN: 1540898881
ISBN-13: 978-1540898883

CONTENTS

DEDICATION

Visits with Doris have touched my heart and given me profound insights into otherwise ordinary things. Her resilient attitude has given me a concrete example of trusting God through the joys and hardships in life. I count knowing her as one of my greatest privileges.

INTRODUCTION

When considering how I would share the stories within this book, my editor and daughter in law, Ashley, offered me a book of vignettes from her personal library as possible inspiration.

In *The House on Mango Street,* Sandra Cisneros describes her younger self when she was a beginning author. It was within the pages of this description that I found the answer I had been looking for, and the exact expression of what I hope this book might mean to you, the reader. *"She thinks stories are about beauty. Beauty that is there to be admired by anyone, like a herd of clouds grazing overhead. She thinks people who are busy working for a living deserve beautiful little stories, because they don't have much time and are often tired. She has in mind a book that can be opened at any page and will still make sense to the reader who doesn't know what came before or comes after."*

I want that for you in your busy life. I want you to be able to pick up this book and find that any chapter can become a poignant moment in your day. If you look for your own life within these pages, perhaps you will find a thread of wisdom to weave into your circumstances.

I continue to stand in awe of the people whose real life experiences were the inspiration for this fictional story. They have lived eight or nine decades plus, and their experiences are archived within their hearts with surprising accuracy. In some cases, when disease has ravaged their abilities, it is the memories of experiences long ago that remain intact. The wisdom gleaned from those experiences is profound and to listen intently would make us rich.

CHAPTER ONE

Caprice

"How many people actually love their job? Seriously Reese, isn't this a small price to pay? Besides, it's only for six months." It was a gorgeous day, and they were enjoying lunch on the outdoor patio of a restaurant near the office.

"Easy for you to say. You were there when the sign up sheet first went around. I would have loved one Saturday morning a month, like you got. Instead, I ended up with one hour *every* week!"

"Oh, Reese, quit complaining. Besides, Mike is letting everyone off early one Friday a month as a thank you. How great is that?" Caprice was nice to work with, but truth be told, she was only happy when all was right with her world. She was the first to whine when circumstances didn't work out the way she wanted. In this case, she was happy because she was one of the first employees to see the slots available and snatched a prime time slot with little commitment.

"So, tell me again, how exactly was this program chosen for our office?" Reese had been out a few days with the flu and missed the staff meeting when the vision for this volunteer program was cast. She felt like the last person to join a party after it was going strong.

"Okay, well, Mike decided that our agency needed a little more exposure in the community. He doesn't think our monetary donations get our name out there enough, so he did some searching for local volunteer stuff and found this. He loved it because number one, it's a national outreach sponsored by one of our clients, and number two, no other ad agency in town is doing it." Caprice was talking fast with lots of enthusiasm. Apparently, her Saturday assignments would consist of painting, weeding, and other occasional improvements for the facility. Reese wondered how enthusiastic she'd be by the third month.

"Okay, I get that, but the program is called Adopt a Neighbor. Couldn't we have helped in the schools or painted a community center or something?" Reese knew Caprice couldn't do anything about it, but she needed someone to hear her out. After all, the other employees probably had their say at the meeting. And for the first time since working there, she felt disregarded.

"Yeah, I asked that. Mike said several schools have already been adopted through other programs, and he wanted us to be different. He feels it will help us stand out. I guess he's already working on media coverage and is ordering t-shirts for us to wear. Oh, I almost forgot. I was supposed to ask you what size you want."

Caprice was clueless as to why Reese was annoyed. Plus, Reese knew that if she said too much against the program, it might get back to Mike. He was a great director and for the most part, she liked working for him. She didn't want him to think she wasn't a team player.

"A medium is good. Caprice, I just wish you would have called me at home and let me know about this. I mean, maybe then I might have had a few choices to pick from."

The truth was, Reese wanted nothing to do with the volunteer assignment she ended up with.

"I'm sorry. I just didn't think much about it. We were pretty busy at work, and it didn't cross my mind to call you. Who knows, Reese? You might end up liking your assignment."

Yeah, right, Caprice. Like I'm gonna like visiting nursing home residents I don't even know. For one solid hour every week! "Do you think there might be times when you'd switch with me? You know, I could take your Saturday and you could take my hour in the week. It would mean a lot to me."

Caprice shrugged. "Maybe. I mean, maybe once in a while. Why don't we just see how it goes?"

Reese knew deep down that her friendship with Caprice was really more surface level and good for things like lunches together. But that was about it. She doubted Caprice would ever switch with her. "Yeah, I guess we'll just have to see how it goes."

As soon as they were back from lunch, Reese called her husband for a quick sanity check. After explaining the situation without taking a breath, she finally inhaled and asked him, "Am I out of line here? I mean, should I really be expected to fulfill this when I didn't even have a say in it?"

"I know what you mean. It does suck. But at this point, babe, you might just have to try and make it work."

"Not what I wanted to hear. Do you think I should talk to Mike about it?"

"Sure, if you think that would help. But just be careful you don't come off sounding like a whiner. Not that you would, I'm just saying."

Reese kept an eye on Mike's office over the next hour. His office did not have a door and two of the walls were glass panels, so it was easy to see when he was available. He didn't look overly busy and Reese wanted to address it now. She rehearsed a few thoughts in her head and then walked across the small lobby to Mike's office entrance. She knocked on the glass and said in an upbeat tone, "Hey Mike, do you have a minute?"

"Yeah, sure, what's up?" Mike was easy to approach about anything work related and was equally easy to problem solve with. But this felt different. This volunteer program had been his idea and one that Caprice said he was fired up about. Reese needed him to see her point of view without insulting his idea.

"Well, since I was sick last week when we had the marketing meeting, I just wanted to touch base with you about the Adopt a Neighbor program."

"Oh, good. Yeah, I think it's going to be great exposure for us in a way that no other agency is doing. Did you get signed up?"

"I did, yes. The sheet had already been around to everyone while I was out sick, so I signed up for the only slot left." Reese shrugged with a smile, hoping her good-natured tone would work in her favor.

He looked a bit concerned. "Gotcha. What slot was it?"

"Oh, it was the visiting slot for an hour a week. If I remember right, any weekday that worked was fine as long as it was an hour." Reese tried to sound indifferent.

"Okay. So is that going to be a problem?" He sat back in his chair, closed his laptop, and looked thoughtfully at Reese.

Here goes. "No, it's not a problem fitting it into my schedule. I can make it work. And I think your vision to adopt a place no one else has, is cool." Reese hesitated. "But to be honest, I just can't picture myself spending one-on-one time with seniors that I've never met. I'm not very good with old people, so those who are in a nursing home seem like a gigantic stretch for me. If we could find a different slot, or if you knew of someone who wouldn't mind switching with me, I'd really appreciate it." *There. That sounded good. He'll understand.*

Mike nodded his head and just said, "Hmm." He pursed his lips and swiveled his chair, like he always did when he was deep in thought. "I tell you what. I'd like you to give this a shot. It's a stretch for a lot of us. But we're going to meet after the first month and get everyone's input as to how it's going. If you're really miserable, let me know at that meeting and we'll figure something out, ok?"

Reese's heart sank. "Seriously?" She shook her head and didn't try to hide her disappointment. "Fine, whatever. Thanks, Mike." Reese had been certain that Mike would understand and reward her good work reputation with a promise to change her slot.

"Reese...knowing you, you'll be fine. Give it a chance." Mike smiled his famous "dig in and get it done" smile. It was one of the only mannerisms of his that she hated. She nodded and smiled back with her lips tightly closed, hoping he could tell she wasn't happy.

Back at her desk, Reese quickly texted her husband, Evan. *Talked to Mike. Can't get out of it. This sucks! Now what?* She tried to get back to work and take her mind off of Mike, Caprice, and the cloak of feeling disregarded. But all she could do was imagine herself in the nursing home, attempting to talk with some elderly person that she had nothing in common with. One thing was for sure, at that first review meeting, she was getting out of it no matter what.

It was hard to concentrate on her work. The whole thing just seemed so unfair. *There have got to be a million other volunteer opportunities and Mike chooses this...for six months!* Reese looked at her calendar and thought about the next six months. She figured that if she planned vacation or sick days a few times it would whittle the number of nursing home visits down to twenty. *Twenty? I might as well work there!*

That night at home, she and Evan were watching one of their shows and talking about it.

"Do I sound crazy to be so upset about this, Evan?" Reese really wanted to know.

"No babe, I mean, it's kind of cool that Mike chose something most employers wouldn't. But to only ask one employee for a weekly slot like yours while the others do one Saturday a month, is definitely lame."

"Thank you." Reese always ate when she was stressed and she was now down to the bottom of her carton of ice cream. "And then Caprice was like, 'Oh stop complaining Reese, at least we're getting paid by Mike for our hours.' And I'm thinking, yeah well if you were in my shoes you'd be causing all sorts of drama over it."

"Caprice is about as immature as they come. Why do you bother with her?"

"Because sometimes she can be a lot of fun."

Evan shrugged. "She's the type that's only fun when she's getting attention. Just wait until she's painting some nursing home room on a Saturday morning."

Reese laughed. "That's true. Maybe she'll actually switch with me once in awhile after a few Saturdays like that."

"Yeah and you never know what everyone else will say at that follow up meeting. Mike might get a lot of push back and decide to go with something else."

"Maybe. Let's hope so. I feel gross after eating this whole thing."

"I'm shocked. Max would have gladly helped you finish it up." Their black cocker spaniel sat faithfully near their feet, wagging his tail as if in agreement.

Evan shook his head and jumped down on the floor. He leaned his back against the couch in front of her and asked nicely, "Please?"

"Ugh, fine. But then I get one after you."

"Of course," Evan agreed knowing full well that might not happen. Reese began to give him a shoulder massage.

"Hey I think you should give me a rub like this the night after every one of my nursing home visits. I'm going to need it."

Evan had his head down, chin resting on his chest, stretching as she rubbed. "I thought you liked old people," he mumbled.

"I like our old relatives, Evan. There's a big difference. What kind of small talk am I supposed to make? I mean, what if they can't even converse? Then what?"

"Then, I guess, you go back to work and get paid for trying. I don't know."

Reese didn't feel like Evan understood what she was up against. She had never before felt disregarded at work. That was part of it, too. Her thumbs dug deeper into Evan's shoulders.

"Ouch! Hey Superman, go easy would ya?"

"You know what? I'm just going to bed." She left Evan on the floor and the empty carton of ice cream on the table. As Reese headed up the stairs, she heard Evan sigh heavily.

"Goodnight Reese," he called out after her.

She didn't answer.

CHAPTER TWO

Lydia

"Ask for Kelly." Mike tossed a nursing home brochure on her desk and turned to leave her office.

"Excuse me Mike, ask for Kelly for *what*?" Reese wanted to act like she didn't know what he was talking about.

"Come on, Reese. Saturday was our first volunteer day at Oak Hills and it was great. We cleaned out an activity center and hauled away boxes of junk for them. Today's Wednesday, so I figured you probably need to get over there before the week's out."

Reese nodded and looked down at the brochure. "Yeah. Okay." Mike didn't stay to discuss it. He was already headed back to his office and Reese knew she had to start today or tomorrow at the latest. "I might as well get this over with." She picked up the phone, called Oak Hills, and asked for Kelly.

"Your first visit will be spent with me. I'll give you a tour, go over the volunteer guidelines, and answer any questions you may have about spending time with our residents." Reese was relieved. "And then if we have time left, I'll introduce you to a few of our Oak Hills friends."

"Hmm. What days do you have available?"

"How about today? I've got plenty of flexibility in my schedule today." Reese already resented how perky Kelly sounded.

Reese didn't want to start today or any day for that matter. But maybe Mike would see that she was willing to follow through if she made the effort sooner than later. "Well, today's not great, but I might be able to make it work after 1:00 p.m."

"Perfect! Just stop by the Activity Office anytime after 1:00 p.m., ok?" Kelly said cheerfully.

"Ok. Thanks." Reese hung up and decided that Kelly had way too much enthusiasm. "*Perfect. Just stop by the Activity Office anytime,*" Reese mocked with a sappy voice and sarcastic expression.

One o'clock came quickly, and Reese pulled into the Oak Hills parking lot. She was surprised at how nice the grounds were. There were beautiful flower gardens and manicured lawns. A few of the residents were outside, blankets over their laps, sitting in their wheel chairs close to the entry. One of them greeted Reese as she walked past.

"Hello," Reese answered as kindly as she could muster.

She signed in at the Guest Center and was directed to Kelly's office. Passing through the atrium, she paused for a moment to take it in. The warm sunshine streamed through the skylights, filling the lounge with warm light, the kind that exudes hope.

Kelly's office was small, but organized. Children's paintings in simple frames were on all four walls. Pictures of her kids were

11

on her desk and on her shelves.

"So your kids love to paint?" Reese tried to open with small talk.

"Yes, but they didn't do any of these. No, all of these were painted by our residents."

Reese was stunned, not only that Kelly would choose to decorate her office with residents' paintings, but that all of their art was haunting in its simplicity and emotion.

The painting directly above Kelly's desk was that of a brown bird with only one wing. It was standing on the ground with black paint strokes all around it. Behind the bird was a tall field of colorful flowers that only made the bird look more alone. The title said, *Free*.

Kelly sat across from Reese, opened some type of manual, and began reading their volunteer guidelines. Reese wasn't really listening. Every time Kelly looked down to read the next guideline, Reese's eyes would search the paintings. The one opposite Kelly's desk had the most realism. It was of a stained glass window, using lots of colors, symmetry, and filling most of the canvas. The title read, *I Can Still See It*.

"Any questions?" Kelly said, quickly bringing Reese's attention back to the task at hand.

"Uh, no. No questions." Reese said quietly.

"Well then, in that case, how about we go on our tour?" Kelly's perkiness was back.

Oak Hills was a large facility with multiple floors, wings, an activity center, and cafeteria. But Reese's favorite part was the atrium. It surprised her just how inviting it was. She wondered why there weren't more people lounging there.

"The atrium is really nice. Is that where I'll visit with residents?" Reese was hopeful that yes was the answer.

"It's possible," Kelly said. "But usually, you'll visit them right in their rooms."

They were headed down the north wing and passed a painter, his drop cloth sprawled over half the width of the hallway. He was covering the cinderblock walls with a color that resembled pineapple left out to turn brown.

"Kelly, what the hell you doin' letting 'em paint the walls this ugly color?" The voice came from behind them. It was a man in his 60's, unshaven, with dirty sweatpants on. He was pushing himself in a wheelchair, stopping to catch his breath.

Kelly smiled and answered him as if he were a child. "Now Dennis, this color's not bad. Besides, I don't get to make those fun decisions."

He looked up at her with a frown. "Then what the hell do you do around here?"

Kelly ignored his question and changed the subject. "Would you like to get past us Dennis? It's a bit crowded with all the painting equipment, isn't it?"

He pushed his wheelchair past them and yelled back over his

13

shoulder. "That's a dumb-ass color. And all you people know it!"

Reese stifled her laughter. She thought Dennis was hilarious. And frustrated. Definitely frustrated.

Kelly acted as if men in their sixties yelling at her was perfectly normal. She stopped outside room 120. "I'm going to introduce you to a woman named Lydia. She's a sweetheart and loves to get visitors." Kelly knocked first. "Lydia? May we come in?"

Knock first. Got it.

"Of course," Lydia replied in a tender voice. She was lying in bed on top of the covers, dressed in a bright purple velour hoodie, pants and big dangly earrings. Her dark, curly hair was up and off her face with a white headband. "Hi Miss Kelly," she smiled. Reese was shocked. Lydia couldn't have been more than 45 or 50 years old.

"How's it going today, Lydia?" Kelly asked.

"Oh, I can't complain," she replied sweetly.

Can't complain? You're young and in a nursing home.

"Lydia, this is Reese. She's a new volunteer here at Oak Hills. I'm showing her around today."

"Hi Reese. It's nice to meet you." Reese just smiled and wondered why on earth this woman was here. She had no intention of asking.

"Lydia's been with us for, what Lydia, about four years?" Kelly asked, still smiling.

Lydia looked straight at Reese. "I have MS," she said. "It got really bad the last few years and my family," she paused to take a deep breath, "just couldn't take care of me." Kelly went on to say that Lydia was diagnosed in her late 30's and had spent the last several years here.

Lydia's voice was soft and winded. It took her awhile, but she went on to explain that her husband passed away four years ago of a heart attack. He had been the only one strong enough to help her at home.

"Lydia used to be an aide for Social Services," Kelly said. "Lydia, you have so many great stories, why don't you tell one to Reese?"

No, not necessary. Let's just go and leave this poor woman alone.

Lydia looked down into her lap, closed her eyes, and chuckled. "Did I ever tell you 'bout a boy I took care of named Kenny?" she asked. "He was somethin' else. He was autistic and that's just the way it was. Hmph…he never minded me, but that's ok. My job was to get him out into the community as much as possible. One day, I took him to Dairy Queen, and before I could stop him, he was sittin' on some strange man's motorcycle in the parking lot. That man was mad, too. I just said, 'Mister, you got to understand, this boy don't know and he don't care.' Lydia giggled. I kinda liked it when Kenny made that man mad."

Lydia went on to share more of her experiences with Kenny,

her brown eyes smiling on her gentle, chubby face. "One day, I had to stop home to get somethin'. Kenny was with me, and he wouldn't take his feet off the dash of my car. My husband stood at the curb, shakin' his head. 'Lydia, for the life of me, I don't know why you put up with that boy.' I told him straight out, 'Baby, I don't see race, I don't see a label, I just see a need. And I'm gonna fill that need, oh yes I am.'"

Reese's eyes filled with tears listening to Lydia struggle to breathe when she talked. Apparently, her disease had affected her lungs as well, and she needed to stop every few words to take a deep breath. The cadence between Lydia's words and her gasps for breath, hung in the air.

"'Lydia, for the life of me, I don't know why you put up with that boy.' (deep breath) I told him straight out, 'Baby, (deep breath) I don't see race, I don't see a label, (deep breath) I just see a need, and I'm gonna fill that need, (deep breath) oh yes I am.'"

Reese stared at Lydia's satisfied expression. Obviously, she found joy in telling it. But Reese had seen enough. She wanted to go.

"Kelly, I don't mean to interrupt, but unfortunately I'm going to have to get back to work. It was nice to meet you, Lydia."

"You're right, Reese. We do need to move along. We'll be back another day, Lydia."

Reese had already turned and was heading out of the room. She waited in the hallway for Kelly and wasted no time telling her she had to go. "I appreciate your time today, Kelly, but I have to be careful not to let these volunteer slots actually go past an hour or I'll get way behind at work. Sorry."

"No problem. I understand. Does this time work well for you next week?"

"You know, I'm not sure. Why don't I just call you?" Reese was trying not to be rude, but she couldn't wait to leave.

"That's fine, but just one last thing. Every visit, we ask our volunteers to make a few notes in a file that we provide. You know, just a few words about how the visit went, what you may have noticed about a resident that you should bring to our attention, things like that. Before next week, could you take a minute to fill this out?" Kelly handed Reese a manila folder.

"Of course. Well, take care." Reese tucked the manila folder under her arm and headed toward the atrium and exit. She checked her phone. She was already 10 minutes over her hour of volunteer time.

This is not going to work. How can I be expected to switch gears like this during my workday? Seriously, Mike has no clue how hard this is going to be on me.

She called him from her car on the way back to the agency. "Mike? Yeah, I'm on my way back and just wanted you to know that this hour slot might be too hard to limit. Today was introductory stuff and I'm still going to be 20 minutes late." *There. He won't want my workflow to be affected.*

"It's no big deal, Reese. I knew that choosing a care center like Oak Hills would mean some give and take. It's okay. Let's just play it by ear for a few weeks and see how it goes."

Reese wanted to scream. None of her coworkers were having their work days affected.

They were all back at work, making progress on their projects. She swung into the lot, grabbed her stuff and ran into the lobby. On the elevator, she closed her eyes and tried to focus. Caprice greeted her as she rushed through the door.

"Hey Reese, how did it go?"

"Good, really good," Reese said disingenuously, and kept walking. She was not about to show Caprice any of her feelings.

"The project meeting's in ten," Caprice called out behind her.

Reese put her thumb up in the air, keeping her stride. Entering her office felt like the finish line of a race. She plopped into her chair and took in a deep breath. *Good thing I was prepared for this meeting ahead of time.*

The manila folder sat under her purse like a duck out of water. What did Kelly say was in it? Reese decided to take a quick peek. There was a single piece of paper, a white form with two columns. The left column was for the date, residents' names and room numbers. The right column had three questions repeated for every resident on the left.

How would you describe your visit with this resident today?
Do you have any questions/concerns about this resident?
How can we help foster your relationship with this resident?

Relationship? So, maybe they only expect me to meet with a few residents.

"Hey Reese, are you okay?" Kevin, one of her coworkers stuck his head in her office.

"Yeah, of course. Why?"

"I don't know, you just look sort of worried. The meeting should go fine."

Reese stood up and started gathering her things. "Oh no, I'm good. Just…thinking. I'll see you in there."

Focus. If I have to do this once a week, I can't bring it back into the office. The last thing I need is to try and explain it.

Reese was determined to close the past hour in her mind. Before walking out for the meeting, she grabbed a pen and scribbled an answer on the form to all three questions.

Fine. No. Not necessary.

CHAPTER THREE

Florence

Reese decided that Fridays would be best to fit in her volunteer hour at Oak Hills. That way, the majority of her week's work would be done. Whatever was left, could go home with her or wait until Monday.

Last week's start had been hard, but she was determined that from here on, she would take more control. She planned to sign in, tell Kelly that they could only visit two people for perhaps 10-15 minutes tops, and be back at the office before her hour was up. She was sure Kelly would understand.

Determined, Reese found a close spot in the parking lot and remembered to check in at the Guest Center.

"Hi. So you're Reese? Nice to meet you. I'm Candi, Manager of the Guest Center. Kelly said you'd be stopping by today. She wanted you to have this name badge, and in this folder are a few residents that she thought you might enjoy visiting. None of them get many visitors, so you can start wherever you like. There's also the typical form underneath to document your visits. Are you familiar with it?"

"Yes."

"Ok, good. I also want to remind you how important it is to sign in and out here. Your badge can be returned here also. Do you have any questions?"

Okay, I like the system, I like the preparation, I like the order. But where's Kelly?

"Thank you Candi, I appreciate this. But isn't Kelly accompanying me on my first visits?"

"She wanted to, however we're short staffed today so she had to help out on our Friday field trip. But if you have any questions, don't hesitate to ask me."

You know what? I'm okay with that because now Kelly won't be able to keep me too long. I can probably get out of here sooner than I thought.

"Thanks," Reese said, slipping the badge over her head. She opened the folder and was taken back by the long list of names and room numbers. There were two sheets stapled at the top, with approximately thirty names on the first page, and almost twenty on the second. *You mean to tell me that none of these people get visitors?*

Reese had no idea where to start and so she approached the list according to whose room might be the closest to the atrium. Florence Carson's room was #104. That sounded close by. She'd start there.

She found Florence's room easily and hesitated outside the door. *What am I going to talk about? What if she's unable to speak?*

I don't want to do this. An aide walked by and noticed Reese just standing there.

"Can I help you?"

"No, sorry. I'm a new volunteer and wasn't sure if this is Florence Carson's room."

"It is. You can just go on in."

Reese nodded and smiled a nervous smile. She was about to walk in when she remembered that Kelly knocked first on Lydia's door. Reese knocked. "Florence, may I come in?"

"Why yes, please do. Hello, dear. How can I help you?"

So this was Florence. She appeared perfectly coiffed. Her hair was neatly combed and styled, and her clothes looked expensive. She had on tiny ivory earrings and a dainty cross necklace. Although she was maybe 5'1", she was doing her best to stand tall in the middle of the room. Reese smiled to herself, admiring this tiny lady who was so put together.

"Hi, my name is Reese. I'm a new volunteer here."

"Well, that's lovely dear. I'm afraid you've caught me doing my chores. I've got to sew a button on this blouse and these newspapers are a mess."

Reese looked around the room. Sure enough, there was a burgundy-upholstered chair littered with newspapers and a sewing kit open on the bed next to a lavender blouse. The bed was made and next to it was a low dresser covered with stacks of books, mostly paperback novels.

"Here dear, let's move these newspapers so you can sit down."

Sit down? How long does she think I'm staying?

"That's okay Florence, I'm fine."

But Florence was already gathering the newspapers and moving them to the bed.

"There you are. Please, make yourself comfortable." She had the kindest look on her face and Reese did not want to be rude.

"Oh, okay. Thank you." Reese obediently sat on the edge of the cushion, her back nowhere near the back of the chair. She didn't want to give the impression that she'd be staying long.

"Kendrick and I brought that chair back from England."

Reese took a moment to inspect the chair. It was a traditional Queen Anne chair, its fabric in like-new condition. "It's very nice."

Florence was gathering a variety of opened envelopes that lay on the same dresser with the books. "Would you just look at all these bills? I guess I know what I'll be doing today. Paying bills." The envelopes looked old and worn, with bent corners, and the top one had writing all over it.

You're in a nursing home. You don't have bills.

Reese ignored the obvious in an effort to connect with Florence. "Yeah, paying bills can take awhile. I'm lucky. I don't have to pay bills. My husband does it."

"Have you met my husband, Kendrick?" Florence asked as she pointed to the other empty bed in the room. It too, was neatly made but there was no dresser, no personal items of any kind alongside it.

"Um, no. No, I haven't."

"Well, he's down in rehab right now. They come and get him pretty early every morning. He's always gone when I get up. Maybe you'll meet him another time?"

"Maybe." *Maybe he's gone because he's not really here to begin with.* "So, you and your husband share a room? That's nice that you can be together."

"Well, yes. He has Alzheimer's, you know. I used to take care of him all by myself, but it just got to be a bit much. Sometimes he wandered from me at the grocery store and the nice manager would find him and bring him back to me. But then one day, no one could find him for a long time. I was so worried. But wouldn't you know, a lovely policeman found him and brought him home. That's when I decided perhaps it would be best to make other arrangements."

Reese just nodded and smiled. Florence was now staring out the window, still standing in the middle of the room with her hands behind her back.

Time to go. "Well, Florence, it was a pleasure to meet you and to sit in such a pretty chair." Reese smiled at Florence, and picked her purse and manila folder up off the floor.

"Kendrick and I brought that chair back from England."

"Yes, yes you told me." Reese was now standing and ready to

wrap up the visit.

"You know, I was married once before I married Kendrick. He was the most handsome man. Something special. He had a lovely job and he took the train to work every day. We had two little boys together and my oh my, we were a happy little family."

Florence had begun to walk in a circle, her hands still behind her back like a tour guide. "Saturdays were our days to spend together with the children. One Saturday, we invited my father to accompany us to the county fair. We had a lovely time. The ride home was hot and the windows were down. Normally, I would sit in the front seat with my husband and the boys would sit in the back. That would be proper, of course. But since my father was along, he sat in the front and I sat in the back between our two boys."

Reese slowly sat back down in the chair, hoping this story would move quickly, and she would find an open moment to excuse herself. Florence continued to walk her paced circle.

"My husband had the radio on like he always did and we were all singing along to the song that was playing. Just then, I happened to look out my window as we crossed an intersection, and saw a car coming fast from the left. We were traveling on a back highway and that oncoming car had a stop sign and was supposed to stop. I tried to yell above the radio, 'He's not slowing down!' but I didn't get it all out before he hit us on my husband's side. It all happened so very fast."

She stopped to look out the window, her expression distant and sad. "My husband and father were thrown from the car but the boys and I were still inside when everything stopped. I couldn't get the car door to open, so I crawled out the window to find them. They were both lying dead on the road."

Reese studied Florence's face. *Could this be true?*

"And so," Florence looked back down and resumed her circle, "I found a job and went to work to raise our boys by myself. And I did fine for several years. I made a life for just the boys and me. Then one day, my mother insisted that I come to the church potluck. Well, I didn't want to go. It was on a weeknight and I was too tired to dress the boys and make a dish to bring. But, I went so she might finally leave me alone about it. And it was there that I met a British man.

At one point in the evening, he whistled at me, which I didn't approve of. So I simply ignored his foolishness. Well, he didn't give up that easily. After the potluck, as I was helping to clear tables, he came up behind me with a tray. I turned around with my arms full of dishes and he slid the tray right under my arms and took the dishes out from under me. Thinking he was heroic, he winked and said something smart in his British accent. Well, I wasn't about to give him any due. So I left him standing there with the dishes and gathered the boys to leave."

Wow, Reese thought, now listening a little closer, *Florence had spunk.*

Florence would go on to describe how she reluctantly accepted a date and then a marriage proposal a few months after that. "Kendrick was the most charming man I ever met. His business was in England and of course I knew accepting his marriage proposal meant that the boys and I would have to move there."

Florence described their home and lifestyle in England in a way worthy of a gifted storyteller. There was a nanny with a white pressed apron and hearty laugh, a large home in the country with a thatched roof and red shutters, and parties with women in long gowns and men in suits with ascots. Even though it sounded like something out of a movie, Reese believed her.

"How long did you live there?" Reese was curious.

"Well, as the boys grew, quite naturally I wanted to come back to the states. I wanted them to have the kind of high schools and sports that I remembered from home. So Kendrick made arrangements and we moved back when the boys were teenagers. My happiness was always most important to him. He gave up his native home for me. And now here he lays in the same room as me and he doesn't even know it." Florence stopped walking her circle and stared at the second bed, empty and perfectly made.

Reese couldn't be sure what was true and what wasn't. But Florence looked so sad and Reese wanted to acknowledge her story.

"Oh, I'm sorry. That must be hard."

Two tears slowly made their way down Florence's petite wrinkled face. She quickly reached for a tissue and wiped the tears from her eyes, took in a deep breath, and resumed her hands behind the back position while lifting her chin high. "That's just the way it turned out. And I have to accept it. It's like my mother always said, 'not everything goes our way.'"

Reese was stunned at her stoic response. Florence regained her composure as if flipping a switch and began to walk her circle again, this time describing the "pale blue satin gown with the white sash and pearl earrings" she wore to one of their parties back in England.

Reese couldn't decide if Florence was strong and determined, or emotionally crippled.

Just then, a few loud, drawn-out moans came from the hallway. Florence stopped to listen and turned to look at Reese, her finger pointing towards the door. "Now that is a lovely man who simply needs to exercise his lungs whenever possible."

Reese grinned. Not only was Florence a gifted storyteller, but a diplomat as well. Maybe she had learned such gentle social graces in England.

The moaning continued and Reese used the opportunity to end their visit. She stood once more, this time determined to leave. "Thank you for allowing me to visit you, Florence. I'm sure I'll see you again some time."

"Well now, that would be just lovely." The light streaming

through her window had dimmed somewhat since Reese arrived, and Florence's tiny frame looked even more fragile than before.

Reese walked out slowly, turning to offer Florence a smile before closing the door behind her. But Florence was already holding the opened envelopes, looking down at them intently.

Reese was anxious to get as far from the moaning man as she could. The atrium was close by and filled with sounds of other people's conversations and instrumental background music. She chose an unoccupied chair in the corner that looked inviting and decided to fill out her required form immediately. Reese liked to get things like that out of the way. She pulled it out of the manila folder, expecting to answer the three familiar questions quickly.

How would you describe your visit with this resident today? Pleasant. Florence is a lovely person. Reese smiled at the thought of using one of Florence's favorite words.

Do you have any questions/concerns about this resident? Reese had several. For instance, was Kendrick really a resident in Florence's room? Did her father and first husband really die in that tragic car accident? Did she really live in England, and come to think of it, where are her grown boys and do they ever visit her? But Reese asked none and simply wrote, *Not at this time.*

How can we help foster your relationship with this resident? Reese hesitated. With as many residents as were on that list, she couldn't possibly initiate relationships. Yet Reese never backed away from completing an assignment. She needed to come up with a satisfactory answer. *Please advise if Florence requests to see me.*

Reese checked the time. Twenty-five minutes left. Based on her experience in Florence's room, she didn't want to get caught in another visit that couldn't be kept short. This week she wanted to arrive back at work on time, if not early. Satisfied with her decision, Reese took out her iPad and checked her work schedule. No meetings this afternoon.

Now relaxed, Reese opened her notes app and checked a few other things. Her mind drifted back to Florence and her remarkable story. On impulse, she opened her journal and typed.

Most people tend to embellish their personal stories. But what if they're older and have dementia? Are their stories true, fabricated, or a little of both? Do they feel as strongly about things in general or do they forget they're in pain, or angry, or lonely? Do they remember casual relationships or new people they meet?

Reese looked up and studied the atrium. The furniture was fairly new with well-coordinated, cheerful fabrics. Shiny, honey colored wood flooring surrounded the lush carpeted center like a fence. Comforting music played in the background and a small, but impressive bird sanctuary was on display in the very center of the space. The opposite end boasted beautiful French doors with colorful stain glass patterns, making an inviting entrance to the dining room. Healthy ferns fell gracefully over the edges of deep blue glazed pots. It really was its own little refuge.

Reese glanced back at the hallway she had come from, lit

only by its florescent lights. The corridor pictures were scarce and rather faded. The walls changed to cinderblock and the flooring no longer coordinated with its surroundings. It was as if the atrium was an isolated world of beauty, surrounded by dreary wings with stagnant rooms.

She turned back to watch the birds, fluttering about in their little glass sanctuary. They were colorful and interesting to watch, but not free.

CHAPTER FOUR

Eleanor

Fridays came quickly, as they usually did for so many reasons. But these past few Fridays seemed closer together for Reese. As she pulled into the nursing home parking lot, it felt as if she had just left. She had a sinking feeling that wouldn't change.

At least she knew what to expect now. She would sign in at the Guest Center and get her badge and list, complete with Kelly's beloved manila folder. She would choose one or two names, visit, and fill out their little form. Done. The entire process felt more manageable than she originally thought it would be.

Today's visit was easy to choose, as Kelly had an asterisk by one of the names, Eleanor Lansing. She hadn't designated a reason for the asterisk, but Reese assumed that Kelly was trying to help. Besides, it didn't really matter to Reese whom she saw or why.

She was getting a little more familiar with the facility's floor plan and found Eleanor's room easily. She slowly opened Eleanor's door in order to peek around the edge before announcing her arrival. What she observed tugged at her heart. Eleanor was sitting in a wheelchair, reaching to arrange several dolls on her bed. She lay each one carefully on the pillow, primped their clothes, and then moved them again.

Reese was surprised at the empathy she had for Eleanor. Was this really the only thing she could think to do with her time? Besides, what was an elderly woman doing with dolls on her bed? "Eleanor, may I come in?"

Eleanor looked around and squinted. "Who's there?" she asked.

"My name is Reese. I'm a volunteer here and I came by for a visit."

"Oh. Sure. Come on in." Eleanor pointed to her bedside table and asked, "Would you bring me that little white box?"

Reese obliged and handed the box to Eleanor, who opened it and turned the box towards Reese so she could see its contents.

"This is the locket my Ernie gave me. Would you help me put it on?"

Awe, how sweet. She wants to wear the locket her husband gave her.

Smiling, Reese obliged, complimenting Eleanor on the pretty pink and silver heart-shaped locket. She gingerly placed it around her neck.

"When did he give this to you?" Reese asked, watching Eleanor stroke the silver engraving of the locket with her fingertips.

"Oh, a long, long time ago," Eleanor replied. "I wear it every day. I miss him so."

Eleanor was a large woman, perhaps in her late 80's. Her short, white hair was in dire need of styling and she looked uncomfortable in her wheelchair. Her right shoulder was higher than her left and her hands were stricken by one of the worst cases of arthritis Reese had ever seen.

As if reading her mind, Eleanor held out her hands with palms down, "I can't put my locket on anymore with these crippled hands." The knuckles were swollen and not one finger was straight. Reese wondered how often and how much those hands must hurt.

"You married?" Eleanor began.

Reese held back a giggle and answered, "Why yes Ma'am, I am." She was amused at how uninhibited Eleanor seemed. Maybe she no longer cared to filter her words or maybe her social graces were just rusty.

"How many years?" Eleanor probed.

Reese smiled, "About three."

She could tell by Eleanor's blank expression, that she was not impressed. "Mmm. We were married for 56 years," she said, shaking her crooked finger at Reese.

Clearly, this trumped Reese's three and she sensed how proud Eleanor was of her marriage. "Wow, that's wonderful."

Reese looked around the room for a place to sit. The corner chair was covered with newspapers, paper napkins, and a worn pair of slippers. If she were going to stay, she would have to sit on the bed, which seemed like an intrusion of private space.

"Eleanor, would you mind if I sat on your bed during our visit?"

"Oh, sure. I wish I had some furniture. But they don't let you bring it. All I have from home is my Ernie's dresser and our nightstand."

Reese couldn't imagine leaving her apartment and all of the things she loved behind. She and Evan found most of their furniture at resale shops or garage sales and transformed them into colorfully painted pieces. Sometimes they would spend an entire Saturday painting, sharing a bottle or two of wine as they worked.

Reese looked around for something in the room that would serve as a conversation starter. On the wall above Eleanor's bed was an aged picture of a young man with blonde hair wearing a sailor's uniform. "Is that Ernie?"

"Yup, that's him, right around the time we met. My girlfriend was going to see her sailor beau and invited me along on a double date. She asked her beau to invite his buddy to come with us. Well, Ernie was that buddy."

Eleanor stared at his picture. "He was darn good to me. A wonderful husband, good father, good provider. If he hadn't come along when he did, I'm not sure what would have become of me."

What would've become of her? At that point, Reese was intrigued and wondered if she should press Eleanor for more details. An awkward silence followed, Reese thought it best to change the subject.

"Are those your children?" she asked, pointing to a few other pictures on the wall.

"Mmm-hmm. Three sons and one daughter. Our daughter lives in town and comes to see me once in awhile. She's got an important job and three kids to take care of."

Eleanor made it sound as if visiting her wasn't as important as her daughter's job and kids. For reasons she wasn't sure of, that bothered Reese. "And where do your sons live?" Reese asked, thinking it was the next logical question.

"Our youngest lives in Florida, our oldest lives out east, and our middle boy…well, he's been dead for ten years." Eleanor's face was serious, her brow furrowed.

"Eleanor, I'm so sorry that you lost your son."

Her steely little eyes stared back at Reese and she said with a cold tone, "I will never, ever, for the life of me, understand why he was cremated and my daughter in law had his ashes spread across the desert where he rode that damn motorcycle."

Reese stared at Eleanor and had absolutely no idea what to say. She waited as Eleanor blew her nose with a napkin she had tucked in her sleeve. Reese couldn't imagine how it felt to lose a son, much less to feel powerless as to the manner he was put to rest.

Eleanor tucked the napkin back in her sleeve. Her eyes went back up to the place where Ernie's picture hung. It was as if looking at him calmed her. She sighed and closed her eyes. Reese hesitated, trying to think of a polite reason to end the visit.

"Before I met Ernie," Eleanor paused with her eyes still closed, "I was going with a boy named Henry who came to see me every Saturday. He lived a good ways away, so he would take the train to see me and I would pick him up at the station. He stayed the weekends at our home and we'd go dancing or take long walks. Sometimes he helped Papa in our barn. He was always making me laugh. I loved him dearly and I knew he was going to ask me to marry him. But I was worried, because he was Roman Catholic and Papa and Mama were staunch Lutherans. I didn't really want to become a Catholic. And he never said if he wanted to become a Lutheran, so I wasn't sure what would become of us."

Is she kidding? So what if they went to different churches? Apparently, it had been an issue; one that Eleanor saw no need to explain.

"Well, before asking me to marry him, Henry was called off to the war. We agreed to talk about marriage after he got back. So we wrote letters back and forth for over a year. I would read them over and over again and keep them in my nightstand so I could reach for them in the middle of the night if I couldn't sleep. Those letters kept both of us going.

But the following summer, his letters stopped coming. I was so worried. Finally, a letter arrived from Henry's sister telling me what had happened. A man from the government came to their door one day and gave them the news that Henry was killed in France in some kind of plane bombing. He was taken all the way to the base hospital, but they couldn't save him. And that's why my letters stopped."

Reese could see the sadness that still gripped Eleanor after so many decades. It was clear she had really loved Henry. "How did you ever get over it, Eleanor?"

Leaning forward in her wheelchair, she whispered to Reese as if telling a secret.

"You never forget. *Never.*"

Reese nodded slowly and waited while Eleanor blew her nose once again.

"Good thing my Papa watched out for me. He knew my heart was broken and he never let me out of his sight. I just wasn't right for three more years and Papa knew it. Some days, I just took off on long walks and he'd come looking for me. When he found me, he'd put his arm around my shoulders and say, 'Sugar, one day the sun's gonna shine again.' Then came the day when I met Ernie."

Eleanor reached for her locket and stroked it. Reese couldn't imagine losing Evan. She was sure that if she ever did, her soul would be crippled like Eleanor's was when Henry was killed. It was something she had never contemplated before.

Reese looked back up at Ernie's picture. It was in a sepia tone with lips and eyes barely enhanced; the color had faded. "He had a great smile, Eleanor. No wonder you fell for him."

"I know it. Believe me, fifty-six years flew by. Better appreciate what you have while you have it," she warned and pointed her finger once more at Reese, with authority.

"Yes ma'am, I will."

One of the volunteer tips that Kelly had impressed upon Reese, was the importance of touch; a hand on a shoulder, a quick hug, and a warm handshake were all encouraged. Reese hadn't planned on touching anyone. Yet Eleanor had just shared a story that changed her life's direction and Reese felt the urge to acknowledge its value. She gently took Eleanor's crooked, swollen hand in her own and said, "Eleanor, thank you for telling me your story. May I come visit you again?"

Eleanor reached for Reese's other hand. She gave them both a squeeze and smiled, "Of course you can, honey. I like visitors."

For some strange reason, Reese wanted to stay. She wanted to hear more about Henry, about Ernie, and about Papa. But that seemed too awkward for a first visit. Maybe there would be a next time.

After leaving Eleanor's room, Reese walked past a vending machine with appealing pictures of cappuccinos. A vanilla latte sounded good. She bought one and went in search of a nearby spot to enjoy it. Just ahead was a turn in the hallway with a little couch by a window. Plopping down, she sat sideways and tucked her feet under her legs. Sipping her latte, Reese stared out the window, reflecting on Eleanor's story. She felt the same way she did after a good movie, except there was no one with her right now to talk about it.

Reese closed her eyes and imagined Henry getting off a train and embracing a waiting Eleanor. Then she imagined Eleanor going to her mailbox the day that letter came from Henry's sister. She could see Eleanor reading the letter while sitting on her front porch. She was sobbing and clutching the letter to her chest.

Although Eleanor talked mostly of her devoted marriage, it was the tears in her eyes when she talked of Henry that intrigued Reese more. She was captivated by Eleanor's story; one that must be true of so many loves lost to war. In that moment, she wanted to somehow pay tribute to their loss.

Comfortable in this cozy spot, Reese checked her time. She had 20 minutes or so before she had to head back to the agency. She wanted to stay in this moment and explore the fact that unexpected events, even a letter, sometimes shove people into a new reality.

Is that true of my life? Losing Nadine felt radical enough.

Reese pulled her iPad from her work tote, wanting to write something that connected Eleanor's life with her own. She waited, with her fingertips poised on the keyboard. She felt compelled to write words that meant something, that held potential truth. The vision of Eleanor weeping on her porch, hugging the letter, birthed the words. And with only one sentence staring back at her, she opened it in her heart slowly, like a heavy door.

Maybe it's true — that we have power over absolutely nothing.

CHAPTER FIVE

Dennis

"You were awfully quiet at the meeting this morning." Mike was standing at Reese's office door. "Got a minute?"

Like I'm gonna say no to you.

"Sure Mike, absolutely."

He sat in one of the two chairs across from Reese. Resting his elbows on the arms, he brought his folded hands up to his mouth, and covered his lips with them. After an awkward silence, he pointed both index fingers at her and said, "I want to know how you're really feeling about our involvement at Oak Hills."

After five weeks, my input is finally regarded?

"You know Mike, I was quiet at the review meeting because I'm at a point of indifference with our involvement there. You see the value in Adopt a Neighbor and I do too. As you know, I didn't appreciate the volunteer slot I ended up with and it's still requires me to really change gears on a Friday. But, I'm adjusting."

"So...you *like* it?" He had a coy smile and Reese couldn't help but laugh.

"I didn't say that. But I guess I don't mind it terribly...for right now."

"Am I going to have a disgruntled Reese if you keep this volunteer slot?"

She knew Mike was trying to give her the out she had asked for five weeks ago. But for reasons she couldn't explain, she wanted to see it through.

"No, you're not. If I begin to hate it, I'll let you know. But I don't foresee that happening." She was softening to her boss's concern and to the thought of her Friday visits.

He smiled and got up to leave. "I like my slot, too. Lexi and the girls have been joining me there on Saturdays and it's been good for our family."

Good for our family. Has it been good for me, too?

"Yeah, I have to admit it's been surprising."

"Told you." Mike winked with his all-knowing expression, the same one he wears when a client is thrilled with a presentation.

Reese just rolled her eyes and shook her head. "I'll see you at the 3:00 meeting."

Mike left happy. It was almost lunch and she wanted to grab a quick bite before heading to Oak Hills. She was going to experiment today with trying to get two visits in, instead of just one.

Once in the car, Reese was feeling confident. *Why not choose men's names today?* After all, they might prove to be short visits and her plan for two in less than 45 minutes could work.

She checked in and easily found two men's names and room

numbers to try. The first one was at the end of the west hallway. Reese was sure this would be easy.

As she entered #126, a man in his 60's with an air tank mounted to his wheelchair was rolling towards her. In his lap, were a Coke, a bag of chips, and a Sports Illustrated. His sweatpants and flannel shirt needed washing, and his face looked like it hadn't been shaved in a week.

"Oh, excuse me, were you on your way out?" Reese asked.

"Wow, what a genius." His voice was hoarse and heavy with sarcasm.

"Oh. Ok, I can come back another time then." Reese started to back out of his room.

"Don't bother," he said pushing his wheelchair past her and into the hallway.

Reese stood watching him wheel himself away, somewhat in disbelief.

"You gonna let him scare you off like that?" A friendly looking aide smiled at Reese. She was dumping laundry into a cart. "That's just Dennis. You can't let him get away with his antics. Go ahead. Follow him."

Are you serious? Follow him for what?

"Oh, that's okay. I'm a volunteer here and I was just going to visit with him a minute, that's all." Reese shrugged and had every intention of moving on to a different name.

"Dennis never gets visitors. Not even his wife. He's all bark and no bite. I'll bet he'd love a visit from you." The aide seemed so sure of herself, that it gave Reese a measure of confidence.

Reese hurried down the hall wondering how a visit with this man would ever work. Nonetheless, she had that same feeling she gets when given an impossible client at work. *I can do this. Just watch me.*

She caught up to Dennis and tried to act as casual as possible.

"So, where are you headed?"

He turned the corner and stopped in front of the elevators. "Someplace you can't go."

Reese smiled. "Oh, really? And where is it that I can't go?"

The elevator doors opened and he pushed himself in. "Fine. Suit yourself."

Reese followed him into the elevator and stood behind him so that he could not see her. She took in a big breath, closed her eyes, and let the air out slowly, as she filled her mind with resolve.

Dennis never gets visitors. Not even his wife. Reese made up her mind to give this visit her best shot.

The elevator bell dinged and the doors slowly opened. Dennis rolled out first and pushed his wheels quickly as if determined to ditch her. Reese hurried to his side and pleasantly offered to push his wheelchair so that he could take a break.

"I don't need your help. I don't need anyone's help," he barked.

Reese figured it must be hard for a man his age to stay in a place like this. He couldn't be more than 65 at the oldest. Her

Dad was 62 and still working. She couldn't imagine her father being in the same situation as Dennis.

Dennis got his wheels going at a good speed down the hallway and Reese had to walk quickly to keep up. When he neared the end of the hall, he slowed down and carefully maneuvered the turn to get through the door to the TV room. His wheelchair's footplate scraped the wood on the bottom of the door, leaving a healthy scratch, and he seemed embarrassed by it.

"Damn doorways. You'd think they'd make 'em wider." He pushed his chair back to a spot far away from the others and turned to look out the windows.

Reese found a small chair nearby and pulled it closer to him.

"I didn't ask you to stay," he said sharply.

"I know," Reese replied, ignoring his gruffness. "So, Dennis, do you watch sports?"

He looked at her over the top of his glasses, as if deciding whether or not to answer her. "Baseball mostly."

"I'm a baseball fan, too. My husband and I are big Rangers fans."

No response. His gaze was now on the TV in the opposite corner of the room.

"Which team do you follow, Dennis?"

"Huh?" He finally looked at her.

"I said, which baseball team do you follow?"

"Oh. The Cubs. They're in Chicago."

"Yeah, I'm familiar with the Cubs. They're an institution in the MLB." Reese was determined to get him talking.

"What would *you* know about baseball?" he countered.

"I happen to know a lot about baseball. I've watched it since I was a little girl."

Dennis stared at her with contempt. "Why are you still here?"

Reese ignored the question. "I'm always interested in what people do for a living. What kind of work did you do?"

Dennis didn't smile, but he did sit up straighter in his wheelchair. Reese saw his face soften a little. "I worked for a crane company," he began. "Forty years. We sold cranes all over the world."

"Wow, forty years. You must have liked your job."

He looked her up and down as if deciding if she was worth his breath. "Best damn years of my life."

Okay, Reese. Keep this going. "By any chance, did you travel for your job?"

"Germany mostly. They were a big client and I did maintenance on our rigs."

"Germany? I would love to go to Germany. If you wouldn't mind, I'd really like to hear a little of what it's like there."

Dennis shrugged. "It's, you know… pretty."

Reese nodded. "Did you have time for much sightseeing?"

He shook his head. "Nope. Just time for a few beers. Good beer there."

"I'm glad that you enjoyed your work, Dennis. Not everyone does."

Dennis looked at Reese longer than the usual glance. His face had rugged, deep lines, and behind his black glasses were kind gray eyes. "I loved my job," he said matter-of-factly.

And look at you now. You probably wish you were still working. "Well, your career must have been something to be very proud of."

He just shrugged. "For awhile, I guess. Nothin' lasts forever." He looked down in his lap and started to brush his fingers over one of the stains on his pants.

Reese had compassion for Dennis. Who could blame him for being angry about the physical change that robbed him of the work he loved? Maybe he needed to talk with someone who was genuinely interested. "Just when was it that you retired, Dennis?"

"You ask a lot of questions," he replied with a scowl.

Dennis' breathing was getting labored and she wondered if she was wearing him out. She eyed the oxygen tank mounted to the back of his wheelchair. The air mask rested next to his right leg. She noticed his hand reaching for it, but he didn't lift it to his face. Dennis didn't seem like the type who would want to put it on in front of her.

"You know what, Dennis? I just realized the time. Am I keeping you from lunch or anything?"

He replied weakly this time, a little out of breath. "Doesn't matter. I don't eat the crap they serve here."

Reese smiled and stood up to go. "Would it be ok if I stopped by again sometime?"

Dennis slumped back in his chair and grumbled, "Suit yourself."

Remembering her training, Reese touched his shoulder and let her hand linger there for a moment. "I'll be back Dennis. I'd love to know more about Germany."

"Well, get goin' then," he said and pulled his shoulder forward away from her hand.

Reese stopped just outside the TV room and remembered Kelly's form. The nurse's station was quiet, so she decided to use the counter to write her comments in the volunteer folder. Glancing behind her, she could still see Dennis. Sure enough, he had put on his oxygen mask. She opened the file and wrote: *Visited Dennis Walter today. He seems to get winded easily. Not very interested in visitors.*

Reese slid her iPad out of her bag and took one more look at Dennis. He obviously had been a strong man and a hard worker. But there was no work to be done here and he seemed decrepit and lost.

Her thoughts flowed easily as she typed in her private notes.

I met a man today that made me work harder to converse than I ever have. Yet, it's crazy that I want so much to visit him again. Maybe next time he would let me in. Is it just that he assumes no one cares? I found out that he loved his career. He worked there for forty years. Does anyone work anywhere for forty years anymore? Maybe that's why it became his identity. He used to spend his days fixing cranes all over the world. Now he lifts an oxygen mask to his face all day. I love my work. I'm good at it. But I can't let it define "the best damn years of my life."

CHAPTER SIX

Jeanie

It was a sunny Saturday morning and Reese had an early training session for volunteers. The "crappy slot," as she referred to it at home, was for one hour on Fridays, which she had already put in. Reese wanted to sleep in with Evan and maybe go for a run. They loved their Saturday mornings and tried to keep them free for just the two of them. And giving that up for one more commitment at Oak Hills was definitely not on her agenda.

Evan was still sleeping. She'd leave him a note. Reese loved handwritten notes sprayed with just a touch of perfume. She had seen Nadine leave perfumed notes for Grandpa and thought it was so romantic. "Good morning, Handsome. Forgot to tell you…training session this morning at Oak Hills. Let's run when I get home? Can't wait to spend the day with you." She carefully propped it in front of his phone.

Reese decided to throw on running pants, an old volleyball shirt and a hoodie. She grabbed her tennis shoes and pulled her hair back in a ponytail. Hopefully, this training would be short and she and Evan could still run this morning. He wanted to check out the new farmers market, too.

This stupid volunteer training better be worthwhile. So does that mean Caprice and the others will be there, too?

Reese found the conference room and walked in a few minutes after 8:00. A simple coffee bar had been prepared, although weak coffee in Styrofoam cups was a huge disappointment. About twenty volunteers were milling around, greeting one another and chatting before the meeting. Reese looked for any familiar faces from work. Two guys from the graphic design department were in the back of the room, but no Caprice.

Why am I not surprised? Come to think of it, shouldn't Mike be here too?

"Good morning everyone! Please find a seat so we can start. Thank you for taking time out of your Saturday to be with us today. We value you so much and look forward to sharing this quarter's training tips with you."

Let's just make them quick training tips, okay Kelly?

Reese decided to sit near Aaron and Dave, who had the decency to show up. She made a mental note to ask Mike if attending these trainings were expected. Based on the fact that there were only three of them there, Reese assumed it was one more little detail that no one bothered to tell her.

Kelly's perkiness was consistent, even within the context of weekend training. "Today we're going to take a little time to review important procedures at Oak Hills. We make our residents' safety a high priority and we want to equip you to do the same. So what do you say, let's work together to be a well oiled machine!"

"Tell me this isn't happening," Dave whispered to her. Reese smiled. At least she wasn't alone in volunteer misery.

The next 45 minutes were a test of Reese's ability to act interested. She considered leaving, but the door was at the front of the room, and Reese didn't want her early departure to be seen by everyone. It was Kelly's closing comments that finally grabbed her interest.

"In closing, I want you to be aware that we've admitted several residents recently who were victims of a string of break-ins to elderly people's homes. Some of those people were attacked and hospitalized as a result. They're here while doctors determine if they'll recover or need permanent residence. If you visit or encounter a new resident that chooses to share their victim story with you, please just listen and don't ask a lot of questions. Simply affirm that you are glad they are getting help to recover. I must remind all of you that you took an oath of confidentiality when signing your volunteer contract. Please continue to honor that oath. Thank you and that about does it for today."

Reese was stunned. She hadn't heard about the break-ins. Come to think of it, she hadn't watched much news at all these past few weeks. She and Evan usually relaxed at night while catching up on their favorite shows. *What do senior citizens have that criminals would want anyway?*

She turned to Dave, "Wow, have you heard about the break-ins?"

"Yeah, I saw it awhile ago on the news." He rose to leave. "Hey, I'm definitely turning in work hours for this."

"Yeah, no kidding. I'm outta here. See ya, Reese." Aaron was already following Dave towards the door, stopping only to dump his half-full coffee cup in the trash.

She overheard two older men in the row behind her. "Prescription drugs. All of that for some prescription drugs," he said, scoffing with disgust.

"Excuse me, is that why the break-ins happened? They wanted people's prescription drugs?"

"Yup. Can you believe it? Quite a few of them were beaten too."

Images of Florence and Eleanor flashed through Reese's mind. The thought of anyone hurting them made her sick. Kelly was gathering her materials in the front of the room and Reese decided to find out a bit more.

"Kelly? I'm so sorry to hear about the crimes. Are there any names you can give me and I'll make a point to visit them next week?"

"Sorry Reese, I can't give you names. But I tell you what, when you come next week why don't you focus on 2-East first?"

Reese nodded in understanding and thanked Kelly. She headed toward the lounge, her mind consumed with the vision of an innocent old woman being attacked in her home. *What the hell is wrong with people?*

On impulse, Reese changed direction and headed toward 2-East, her plan to go home and run temporarily forgotten.

She slowly walked the hallway, intentionally looking through each doorway, not sure how she would recognize who may have been victims. Finally, near the end of the hall, Reese spotted a woman sitting alone on her bed; the door was open and the room dark. She read the name written on the dry erase board outside the room. "Jeanie Krane."

Reese knocked first and softly called out her name. "Jeanie?" Nothing. This time a bit louder, "Jeanie?"

Slowly Jeanie lifted her head and looked at Reese. "Yes?" She answered.

Upon first look, Reese was horrified. The tiny, frail woman had bruises and large scabs on her forearms and face. There was a bandage on the back of her head and one eye was swollen halfway shut.

"I'm Reese...a volunteer here. I just came by to introduce myself and see how you're doing."

Jeanie nodded and motioned to a nearby chair. Reese took a seat.

"I just got here." Her voice was so soft and weak that Reese could barely hear her.

Looking around, Reese could find nothing in Jeanie's room

to use for opening small talk. No family pictures, no trinkets, no plants. It was then that Reese noticed how beautifully Jeanie was dressed. Her blouse had a lace collar, her short-sleeved blazer was made of linen, and her pants looked expensive – definitely not polyester.

"Jeanie, you have such a pretty outfit on."

"Oh. Well, you know, I sew. I always have. Sew most all of my clothes. Don't suppose I'll be doing much of that now," she said holding out her badly damaged arms for Reese to see.

"Oh my goodness," Reese said, as if she hadn't seen her arms until now. "What happened to your arms?" *Kelly said no questions.*

"Well….a young man who cuts my grass went a little crazy. He hurt me and I woke up on my kitchen floor. My cat was licking my face."

"Oh Jeanie, I'm so sorry to hear that. What do you mean he went a little crazy?" *Okay, so two questions.*

"Well, he wanted my pills and I told him I was almost out and waiting for more to come in the mail. That's when he got angry and started hurting me. I don't really remember how I ended up on the floor."

Jeanie's words were so matter of fact, and her attitude seemed one of surrender. "When did this happen?" Reese asked, no longer mindful of Kelly's instructions.

"Oh, maybe a week or so ago. I was in the hospital a few days, I suppose. "

"Jeanie, that's just awful. What are you planning to do?"

Reese instantly wished she could have her words back. Most residents were so feeble, so vulnerable, that others usually made decisions for them. Case workers, doctors, family members, all seemed to have a voice. Residents often did not.

"I don't want to go back to my house," Jeanie said sadly. "I think I'd be too afraid there." She ran her delicate, wrinkled fingers over the ugly, purple scabs invading her forearms.

"I can certainly understand that."

Reese found herself daydreaming about breaking down the door of the perpetrator's apartment. She envisioned kicking him, throwing him to the ground, putting his hands in handcuffs, and then stepping on his face until he screamed for her to stop. She saw herself as an action hero, a supernatural cop of sorts, getting revenge for Jeanie.

Jeanie's feeble voice halted her fantasy. "If you don't mind, I think I'll lie down."

"Oh, of course. Do you need help, Jeanie?"

"Will you help get the blanket over me?"

Jeanie's groans as she lay back on her bed gave Reese a chill. She lifted the blanket from the foot of the bed and gently covered Jeanie's legs with it.

Reese whispered, "I hope you're feeling better soon, Jeanie." Her eyes were already closed, and she looked pitiful beneath the faded green blanket.

As Reese walked back down the hallway, her steps got faster and angry energy filled her body. *How is it that some people can be so vile and cruel to others, especially the innocent and weak? If I ever meet the man that did this to Jeanie, I want to see him in pain.*

On the way back to her car, Reese remembered the run she and Evan had planned. She needed it now more than ever. She gave him a quick call while getting in her car.

"Hey, you done?" he answered.

"Yeah, I'm done. I could really use that run. You up for it?"

"Sure. We'll go when you get home, ok?"

"Ok."

"What's wrong, Ree?" Evan knew every tone of her voice and could usually read her mood.

"I'll tell you on our run. I love you. See you soon."

"Love you too."

Jeanie's battered arms and swollen eye were on Reese's mind the entire way home.

How could something so vicious happen to someone so vulnerable?

"Free will, Reese," Nadine would say. "God gave us all a free will, good or bad. That way, we get to choose the good for ourselves."

Nadine's words about free will never sat right with her. Reese felt that if one reflected on something long enough, researched it hard enough, one could come to a reasonable understanding of most anything. But not this. The mystery of crime, natural disasters, and disease all overwhelmed Reese at times. The harder she tried to study them, the more they eluded her.

"Ree, why can't you just accept that some things in life are going to be a mystery?" Evan asked as they ran in the nearby park.

"Because if I accept that, then I'm saying I can't do anything about it," she huffed, grateful to finally feel winded, a welcome release from the frustration within.

"Not really. You're just acknowledging that you can't control it. There's still a lot you can do about it." They ran a little farther on the familiar path, passing walking families and a young girl whose father was removing the training wheels from her bike.

"Once the damage is done Evan, it's not like we can change the outcome," she retorted, getting slightly annoyed with him.

"All I'm saying, is that listening to Jeanie and showing her you cared, was a moment when you *were* doing something about it."

Evan was finally getting winded too, and they agreed to make the turn back toward their neighborhood. He waited until they were walking to bring it back up. "Look Ree, I'm not saying that I have the whole good and evil thing figured out. All I'm saying, is that when we choose to respond to something awful that's happened, we're keeping good going."

Reese glanced at Evan, his hair now wet with sweat, his eyes sincere as always.

She wasn't sure if it was the run or Evan's words that were making her feel better. Either way, her mind was clearing, and she was hungry. "Maybe so. Hey, I'm starved. How about some lunch?"

Digging through the refrigerator, Reese found a few peaches, some leftover chicken, and fresh mozzarella. Evan filled their water glasses, and soon they were enjoying lunch on their apartment patio. The sun was warm on Reese's back, and the sound of a nearby lawn mower was somehow soothing in its normalcy.

"Good lunch. Hey, do you want to get ready and then we head to the market?" Evan loved Saturdays and his goal was usually to fit in as much as possible. "Let's take Max with us, too. He's been indoors most of the week." Hearing his name, Max looked up at her from under Evan's chair. *Yes Max, that cute furry face will get you anything.*

"Definitely." Reese knew it would take her longer to shower and change, but she could never resist an opportunity to sit alone and reflect.

Once Evan left, she closed her eyes and took in a deep breath, lifting her face to the sun's rays. Instantly, she imagined Jeanie on her bed, frail and hurting. But this time, Reese smiled. *And there I am right beside her, keeping good going.*

CHAPTER SEVEN

Rose

Reese needed to pick up a few things from the grocery store on her way home from work. She and Evan were trying a new recipe tonight that she found on one of her favorite blogs. She loved it when they cooked together. They'd usually put on music and open a bottle of wine. Reese would wear Nadine's apron and Evan would usually tease her that it turned him on.

He liked to experiment with new foods and Reese was grateful for his sense of adventure in that way. Except of course, when he'd refuse to measure and simply estimated the amounts of each ingredient. It drove her crazy. Just last week he had sabotaged the French tarragon chicken recipe she had wanted to try for a long time. "Evan, it's not going to turn out if you don't measure exactly," she insisted.

"So what? I'm having fun, Reese. If the recipe doesn't turn out, we'll order Chinese." And then he flashed that huge smile, the one that implied she's trying too hard.

"Come here, Handsome. Why is it that your smile gets you anything?"

Evan took her in his arms. "Define *anything*," he teased.

Reese quickly forgot about measuring, distracted by Evan's broad shoulders. Their last cooking night had ended so romantically.

Reese followed everything in life by the book. Rules, directions, measurements, all brought her considerable comfort. She embraced anything that might help her avoid mistakes. But Evan enjoyed the unknown, even if it was just experimenting with a recipe. Reese laughed just thinking about how opposite they are in that way. True, it was annoying sometimes, but like Nadine always said, "God puts folks together that need each other."

Reese glanced at her car clock. She would be getting home a lot earlier than usual for a Friday. Then it hit her. *For a Friday!* She never went for her hour at Oak Hills today. It had totally slipped her mind.

The House of Fun (as Evan referred to it) was about five blocks from the grocery store. *I've got extra time...I could still fit in a quick visit and fulfill my weekly obligation.* Reese hated loose ends and this felt like a loose end to her. She knew she'd feel better about the weekend if she could cross this obligation off in her mind.

Feeling good about her decision, Reese drove directly there and easily found a close parking spot. She signed in and Candi handed her the infamous manila folder.

"Hi Reese. I thought maybe we weren't going to see you this week."

"Not a chance. Just couldn't make it earlier today." *And I totally forgot.*

Reese looked at the manila folder. It seemed so archaic. Nonetheless, she opened the file and chose the first name on the list. Rose in #107. Sounds fine. She would make a quick, efficient visit and still get home early.

Rose's room made a nice first impression. Her bedspread was pastel tones with decorative pillows in a wildflower pattern. Above her bed, hung an oversized painting of wildflowers on canvas. A modern, white dresser and matching nightstand appeared clean and maybe even new. Several healthy looking plants were on her dresser and windowsill. Reese had yet to see a resident's room that had such an updated look. The only item in the room that appeared to be from the past was a pink crocheted blanket draped across a small reading chair.

"You here to see Rose?" Her roommate had a loud, raspy voice and a scowl on her face.

Reese could have said, "Actually, I'm here to see you." It certainly didn't matter whom she visited at this point but the scowl and raspy voice were far from inviting. Reese hoped that Rose would be a better bet.

"Yes, yes, I'm here to see Rose. Is she busy?"

The hunched over roommate pointed her thumb towards the bathroom and grunted, "She's in there. Good luck waitin' for her. She takes her sweet time with everything."

"Oh. Okay, thank you."

"Is someone here for me?" Rose yelled from behind the cracked open bathroom door.

Reese didn't know what to do. Who knew how long this woman would be in the bathroom and at this point, was she obligated to wait?

She hesitated and then answered, "Yes, I'll just wait."

"Well, who are you?"

Please don't tell me I'm having a conversation with a woman on the toilet. This is so awkward. I could have been at the grocery store right now.

"Uh, I'm a volunteer. I'll just wait."

"Oh, how nice. Don't you worry, I won't let the grass grow. Be right out."

Oh my gosh, I could still get out of here. She's not gonna know who it was that came to visit her. I'm leaving.

But just then, the bathroom door opened and Rose walked out—no wheelchair. She was using a walker and seemed stronger than most residents. She was about the same height and weight as Reese, with curly white hair. Reese was impressed the most by the baseball jersey she was wearing. It was a Mets jersey and an expensive one at that.

"Look out, I can't always stop this thing once I'm going full speed." Rose winked at Reese, who just stared at her and then looked away as not to be rude. "Relax, would ya? I'm just kidding."

Rose plopped onto her bed, trying to catch her breath. She was quite winded for having walked such a short distance. However, she still had the strength to take herself to and from the bathroom. After several months of visits, Reese knew that independent mobility was a big accomplishment for any resident.

Rose's reading chair wasn't littered like other residents' chairs. "May I sit down Rose?"

"Of course!" Rose had finally caught her breath. The roommate with the scowl turned on her TV and fixed her gaze on the screen. Reese felt a tinge of guilt about not including her in the visit.

"So then, tell me about yourself," Rose said, leaning forward towards Reese.

Wait. I'm here to see you and you want to know about me?

"Well, I'm a marketing analyst at an advertising agency nearby and we're volunteering here at Oak Hills as part of the Adopt a Neighbor Program."

"Mmm. Good for you. A lot of people here could use some company. I'm one of the lucky ones. I have a wonderful daughter and son in law who spend a lot of time with me. She redecorated my room. Isn't it beautiful?"

"It is really nice, yes." Rose seemed to have such a positive disposition.

"I love your Mets jersey, Rose. I'm a baseball fan too, although not exactly a Mets fan."

"I know what you mean," Rose tossed her hand down with disgust, "they stink. But wearing their jersey sure beats the old lady type clothing nowadays."

Reese laughed out loud. "I guess so. Do you have other jerseys?"

"Oh, of course. Got a closet full of 'em. It's all I wear. If you don't mind, how's my lipstick?" Rose raised her chin and pursed her lips. "Did I get it on right?"

Rose's lipstick was a bright red and applied too far above her top lip on one side.

"You know, it's a very pretty color, but just a little crooked on this side." Reese tapped her own lip in the same place.

"Hand me that mirror on top of my dresser, would you?" Reese handed her the small mirror.

"Yee gads, that's scary!" Rose began wiping it off with her crumpled tissue.

Reese stifled a laugh.

"I need some earrings on, too," said Rose. "You know, I gotta get with it this year."

"Excuse me?"

Rose smiled and shrugged. "Just because I'm in here doesn't mean I can't have my act together," she said matter-of-factly. "Would you hand me that little white box on my dresser?"

Reese instantly spotted the small, white cardboard box with the worn corners. She handed it to Rose, who opened it carefully and laid it on her lap. Inside, were several pairs of earrings and Rose chose a pair with white centers and blue stones around the edges. She put them on and handed the little box back to Reese.

"*Now* I've got it goin' on," said Rose, checking the mirror once more. "Always remember, lipstick gets you ready for anything." She winked at Reese and handed her the mirror to put back.

This woman is a blast.

"So I see you're married. That's some ring you've got there."

Evan would be pleased that even an elderly woman complimented his carefully chosen ring. "Yes, three years." Reese looked down at her beloved ring, remembering the hopeful look on Evan's face when he gave it to her.

"So, how's it going? Marriages can be tough, especially out of the shoot."

Reese thought Rose was fun so far, but what would a woman her age remember about young marriage? "It's great. He's a keeper."

"Oh. Well, I know a thing or two about keepers. My second husband was, my first one wasn't."

Uh oh. I hope we're not getting into a long story here.

"My first marriage only lasted eight years. Found out he had been cheating on me all along."

"Mmm. That's too bad, Rose."

"No, I learned a lot. You can't marry someone expecting them to cater to how you want everything to be. And the truth is, that's exactly what I did. And he hid I guess, by keeping company with other ladies."

She shrugged and shook her head. "We were both miserable. I was determined to stay in order to keep our family together. I didn't want our daughter to go through the pain of her parents separating. I'm not proud of finally letting go, but it seemed like the only choice left."

Rose explained that their daughter lived nearby. It sounded as if she and her husband were attentive to Rose and always her advocates. "They're just wonderful and believe me, I know I'm lucky. Not many folks here have someone who really wants to see them."

Reese was glad for Rose's sake. But she was still keeping an eye on the time and wanted her to finish her story so she could go.

"And what about your second marriage?"

"Well, let me tell you, I was quite young when I met Oliver. I fell hard for him that's for darn sure. But he planned on doing mission work overseas and I wasn't much of a churchgoer back then. Didn't seem right to pretend that would interest me. And it wouldn't have been fair to him. So we parted ways until much later."

"Did you tell him how you felt?"

"I should have. But no, I didn't. When I finally met up with him again, it was about twenty-five years later. We had both been married and divorced by then. I took one look at him after all those years and felt like I was home."

Reese loved how Rose's face lit up when she talked about Oliver. *Does my face change like that when I talk about Evan?*

Reese couldn't believe how similar the story was to her aunt and uncle's. Her Aunt Julie followed her Uncle Craig to the mission field, even though mission work wasn't even on her radar. They had a rocky start, but as far as Reese knew, they were happily married all these years later. She was so fond of Uncle Craig and understood why Aunt Julie would have done anything to be with him. Maybe Oliver was like him.

"So, what was he like? Oliver, I mean."

"Well for starters, he was handsome but pretended not to know it. He was protective of others. What I mean is, he loved justice. And he could talk to anyone and make them feel special. A big part of our marriage was helping other people. It gave us both such fulfillment."

"Don't you wish things had been different from the start? I mean, it kind of sounds like you two were meant for each other from the very beginning."

Rose smiled and seemed so much at peace. "If it had been different, I wouldn't have my daughter. Besides, I wouldn't have been right for him the first time. He loved God and I didn't. Now I know that the Bible calls that 'unequally yoked'. Or as I like to say, there's trouble on the horizon."

"But you could have had so many more years together," Reese insisted, thinking of Aunt Julie and Uncle Craig.

"Honey, I have no way of knowing what might have happened. We can fill our days with 'what ifs' but it won't change a thing."

Reese was intrigued. She viewed Rose's story as twenty-five years of happiness lost. But Rose considered it an ordained path. *Can the passing of time really give you that kind of perspective?*

Rose just winked at her and readjusted her position to get more comfortable. "So. Tell me about *your* life. Something good. No sense focusing on the bad stuff. Doing that just sends our thoughts downhill."

Reese obliged and told Rose more about her work. As she described her responsibilities, her clients, her team, Reese was feeling pretty good about her job.

In that moment, a grateful feeling rose to the surface and felt as if it were under her skin. Despite her recent complaints, she knew she had a job she loved. But it couldn't be more the opposite for Evan.

"I wish the same was true for my husband," Reese explained. "He isn't working in his field and is terribly bored. Plus, the management is awful. Really awful. But it's been so hard to find anything else that pays what we need."

Rose nodded with an understanding look on her face. "Honey, I know you can't relate to this, but in my day, people did all sorts of work they didn't like just to put food on the table. Myself included. It wasn't fun, that's for sure. But sometimes, work isn't about you. It's a means to provide for others. This world's forgotten that. Try not to fret. My guess is that things will change eventually."

Reese sighed, "I hope so. I just wish I could help change it for him."

Rose's expression looked so kind, so caring. "Honey, a man's work will always be important to him whether he enjoys it or not. You *can* help by thanking him for what he does, for taking care of you both. Telling him you appreciate him is like gas in his tank."

Gas in his tank? Reese really did appreciate Evan's efforts to take care of them. *I've told him that, haven't I? Who is this woman?*

Reese sensed a familiarity with Rose that she couldn't place. "Your turn, Rose. Tell me something good."

Rose held her hand to the side of her mouth and whispered as if telling a secret. "They might move Little Miss Sunshine to another room," and pointed towards her roommate.

Reese burst out laughing. "So, not the best combination, I take it?"

Rose pursed her lips and raised her eyebrows. "Some days chickens, some days feathers," she answered.

Reese made a mental note to tell Evan *that* one. He'd love it. She glanced at the clock on the wall. *Evan...cooking tonight!*

Reese stood up slowly to leave. "Rose, unfortunately, I have to get going."

Rose looked up at her and reached for her hand. Reese let her take it. "Thanks for coming, honey. I loved meeting you."

"I loved meeting you too, Rose."

On her way out to the parking lot, Reese was greeted by the peaceful sound of the outdoor water fountains. She hoped the residents got to enjoy the grounds at some point this week. She especially hoped Rose's daughter would bring her out here.

Once in her car, Reese set her purse on the passenger seat and looked back at the building. Rose was cool. In some ways, she was like Nadine, who had the knack of saying the right things at the right times. Reese wondered how often she could fit visits in with Rose. Maybe it could be an every other week type of thing?

She had intentionally skipped her duty of filling out Kelly's form. That could wait. But capturing this intriguing woman could not. Rummaging through her work tote, she grabbed her iPad and opened her journal.

Rose had experienced two entirely different marriages and yet valued the purpose of both of them. She had done unfulfilling work for the mere privilege of providing. And she wore baseball jerseys! The words came easily to Reese's fingertips.

Almost forgot my volunteer visit today. Would have been a shame to miss meeting Rose. Hope I'm that cool when I'm old. Hell, I'd like to be that cool now! She was positive...and funny! The story of her two marriages isn't all that unusual, but her perspective is. 'You can fill your days with what ifs, but it won't change a thing.' Maybe the passing of time really does have the power to mature your thoughts like that. Apparently, a little lipstick doesn't hurt either.

CHAPTER EIGHT

Monica

Meeting Monica for breakfast was always a highlight for Reese. She felt lucky to live only two hours away from her best friend and they were intentional about meeting every few months, usually on a Sunday morning. They had been friends since high school, and Reese still admired Monica as much as she did when they were seventeen. She was just so comfortable in her own skin.

This particular Sunday, Monica was full of excitement about a new guy she met at a conference. "Ok, so he's gorgeous. Gorgeous! But not in a 'yeah, I know I'm hot' kind of way. He was easy to talk to and just super relaxed. I think that's what I liked most about him, how relaxed he was. You know those guys that are talking to you but at the same time looking past you, like they're watching for someone else? I hate that. Kevin was cool. He actually was focused the whole time. Unbelievable."

Reese was caught up in Monica's enthusiasm and genuinely happy for her. "So what's his last name? I want to check out his profile."

"Here. I'll show you some of his recent posts." Monica grabbed her phone, quickly pulled up a few pictures and handed it to Reese.

Reese gave Monica the exact type of feedback she was hoping for. "Oh, I totally see why he got your attention."

The waitress took their order and assured them they could take up her table for hours and she wouldn't mind. "Seriously," Monica told her, "this might take awhile."

They both laughed, still sharing the same understanding they had with each other since high school. Even though they had attended different colleges, they stayed close, catching up as often as possible. Because of the way their souls understood each other, Reese was convinced their friendship was destined unto old age.

Monica lived an exotic life. She traveled abroad for her job, met interesting people, and attended fancy cocktail parties. Her condo decor continually evolved with beautiful artifacts from all over the world. Nothing in her home matched and that was exactly the way she wanted it.

If Monica liked this new guy, it could only mean one thing. A few amazing dates and then she'd cut it off.

"So, does he stand a chance?" Reese teased.

"Of course he stands a chance. For as long as need be." Monica grinned with her steely confidence and flipped her long, black hair behind her shoulders.

"Oh my gosh Monica, what's your plan?"

"Look, I'm not saying this is gonna be a steady thing. We

already went out that night for dinner and had a fantastic time. He travels. I travel. The odds of our schedules being compatible are nil. So, we'll enjoy it while it lasts and then move on."

That was Monica—beautiful, intelligent, and determined to keep romance at an arm's length. Guys usually loved that about her.

"Ok, so what if it feels like more than that after a few dates?" Reese was always hoping to convert Monica into a romantic.

"Oh please. You know I adore Evan. But there's not that many Evans out there, Reese. Trust me. Besides, there's a time for everything. And right now, my life has no room for a serious relationship."

"Already made the T-Chart, huh?"

"Hey, don't knock it. It works for me."

Raised by a single mother, Monica had been taught to think every situation through on paper. She and her mom would religiously sit down together, draw a T-Chart on paper and write down the pros and cons of whatever decision she was facing. Whichever column had more entries was the decision she went with.

"I know it has and I admire you for it. But take it from someone whose heart steers her in a million directions, yours will too one day."

"Will what?" asked a slightly distracted Monica, as she quickly checked her texts.

"Your heart. One day, it's gonna make those columns on paper seem ridiculous, 'cause you're just gonna *know*," insisted Reese.

"This is why we're good for one another," Monica declared and pointed a finger at Reese, "You make me look up, and I remind you to look down."

Reese laughed. "Yeah, I guess. Promise me you'll give it a few dates with Kevin before you put him on paper. Or have you already?"

"I'm definitely having the veggie omelet," Monica said, changing the subject.

"Then you have." Reese grinned at her strong-willed friend.

The waitress continued to check in on them every so often, as the two covered all subjects they deemed necessary. At Reese's request, they usually talked about one of Monica's recent trips. She was faithful to describe visual details, knowing how much Reese longed to travel. Her most recent trip had been a second visit to Milan.

Monica always managed to negotiate an extra day or two for sightseeing, even when meetings were supposed to dictate her itinerary. "To be honest, the touristy stuff is the least interesting in my book. I always ask the locals what hot spots they love most and then I go visit those."

Of course you do, you're Monica.

"Ok, enough about my trips." Monica knew the line between

sharing and bragging. "You never told me the story of how that volunteer thing went down at work. Did you get out of it? It's been more than a couple months, right?"

"Yup. I know this is gonna sound crazy, but I kind of like it."

Monica stared at Reese with her infamous "what are you thinking" look.

"Here's the thing. Some of the residents are just really sweet. Not all of them, of course, but there's a few that…well, like this one woman Jeanie. She was actually attacked by her lawn guy who wanted her pills. When I met her, one eye was swollen shut, her head was bandaged and her arms were full of bruises and scabs. And Monica, she was this tiny, frail little woman. She can't even sew anymore and that's what she really loved to do. I'm telling you, it made me furious! I wanted to find this guy and beat the crap out of him."

"Yeah, no kidding. That's terrible."

"And then there's this guy Dennis. He has emphysema really bad and wears an oxygen mask a lot of the time. Well, he does this tough guy façade but I think deep down, he wants to connect. He had to retire earlier than he wanted to and it's like he really doesn't belong there. I don't know. I want to see if he'll let me get to know him a little better. He's this dinosaur who actually worked at the same place for like, forty years! And the sad thing is, his total identity was in his work. Which he no longer has."

Monica just smiled at Reese.

"What? Do I have food in my teeth?"

Monica laughed. "No, it's just cool. Your enthusiasm I mean."

"Monica, seriously. These people have amazing stories. This one woman lost the love of her life in the war and then finally met this other guy who she married and loved just as much. But I couldn't help but feel she loved him differently than her first love. Her story could easily be a good chick flick. And then, there's Rose. Oh my gosh Monica, this woman is a trip! My first conversation with her was actually while she was on the toilet!"

Monica's eyes widened. "You're kidding."

"I wish. Then she comes out of the bathroom in this awesome baseball jersey. And she's cracking little jokes about herself. Then she starts asking questions about my life, and was genuinely interested. She wasn't at all self-absorbed in the nursing home way of life."

Reese was talking faster, her affection for Rose painted on her face. "And here's the freaky thing. She reminds me of Nadine. Not in specific ways. There's just something about the way I feel when I'm with her. As if what I want to say is safe and what she'll say back is helpful. I've actually gone back to see her a few times already."

Monica was proud of her dear friend in that moment. "That's so cool. I'm happy for you that it's turned out so well. I mean this whole volunteer assignment could have been a disaster, not to mention a sticking point between you and Mike. Who knew it would turn out to be a joy in your life?"

"Well, I wouldn't go so far as to say a 'joy', but I do kind of look forward to it now."

"Reese, I've known you a long time. And I can tell you're getting really invested in this. Don't you hear the enthusiasm in your own voice?"

Reese's face grew serious and she took in a deep breath. She let it out slowly, while Monica's words still lingered in the air.

"I guess…maybe I am invested." She shook her head in disbelief. "Wow. What am I doing? I've got to be careful not to get too close to these people. I mean, this obligation will be over in a few more months and I can't keep visiting them after that. I don't have time, right? It's totally not practical."

Monica was quiet, using her fork to push around her half-eaten omelet. "Mmm. Why isn't it?"

This time, Reese was the one who got quiet.

"More coffee here?" The waitress held up a fresh pot of steaming hot coffee.

"Yes, please. And could I have some more creamer?"

"Sure. I'll be right back with that."

"I think deep down, I want to keep going for visits. You're right Monica, I am invested. It's just that right now, it's part of my job so it makes sense. But once Adopt a Neighbor campaign is over, do I really want to make time in my week for nursing home visits? Not that they're not important people, it's just weird. I never pictured myself doing that kind of thing."

"Well, what *do* you picture yourself doing? For volunteer work, I mean."

"I don't know. Other than runs for good causes or the occasional soup kitchen thing when I was in my teen church group, I haven't done much volunteering."

"So if you haven't pictured yourself in a certain kind of volunteer role before this, maybe you're hesitant for a different reason."

"Like what?"

"Is it possible that it might have something to do with Nadine?"

Reese scowled and dismissed Monica's suggestion immediately. "No. Why would it have anything to do with Nadine?"

"Look, I know how hard you are on yourself. When Nadine died in that nursing home a few years ago, it killed you that you hadn't been up there to see her. You had so much guilt over it. Maybe…maybe if you keep visiting these people when it's not expected for work, you'll feel like you're giving them more than you gave her."

Reese looked away, watching their waitress clear a nearby table, balancing plates on the inside of her forearm. Her eyes were brimming with tears and she grabbed her napkin before they could run down her face. Why was anger stirring in the pit of her stomach?

"I'm sorry Ree, I know it's still hard and I know she meant the world to you. But don't you think she'd love the fact that you're reaching out to the residents? It kind of rings true with so much of what she modeled, you know?" Monica held her breath, worried that she had gone too far.

Reese kept her eyes down and nodded her head while absorbing the last tear with her napkin. "Yeah. I know. I've just got to think about it."

Reese was still fragile when it came to talking about Nadine and Monica knew she had opened a wound. It was time to change the subject.

"Well, I'll tell you what. I could totally use your help picking out something for my next date with Kevin. I was thinking of checking out Lilly's. Do you want to go with me?"

"Yeah, that'd be fun." Reese was relieved and a little shopping would be a good distraction from the heavy ending to their conversation. They asked for the bill and decided to ride together, with Reese asking questions about the kind of outfit Monica wanted.

She had a contemporary style, preferring solid colors and simple lines. It was never a problem finding something Monica liked at Lilly's, only a problem deciding on which one to buy. Reese convinced her that the bold blue outfit looked best with her dark hair.

"Ok, done. Except now I need earrings 'cause I have nothing that would look good with this." Skimming the earring racks, Monica lifted up a pair that Reese hated. "What about these?"

"Definitely not. They're too gaudy."

Monica bought them anyway, never deterred by another's opinion, not even Reese's.

After shopping and good-byes, Reese was grateful for the long drive home to reflect on their friendship and conversation. Her thoughts skipped around, taking inventory of all she wanted to remember.

I know her. She likes Kevin more than she's letting on. She took a long time picking out that new outfit. I loved what she picked out. But why does she always choose such weird earrings?

Anyway, I love our friendship. She knows me so well. I can't believe she brought Nadine into it, though. Is she right? Do I feel unfaithful to Nadine?

Geez, Milan! Monica went to Milan...again. If she only knew how lucky she is.

I wonder when she'll get married. What if she never does? No...she will.

Are there really not many Evans out there? That can't be true. He is pretty amazing, though.

Did I tell him I'd be later than usual today? Crap, I forgot to text him.

When's the last time I wore a cocktail dress? Who am I kidding?

I'll probably never need to wear a cocktail dress.

I've got to remember to call Monica next Sunday. That date's gonna go well, I just know it.

I hope he doesn't hurt her. No, Monica can take care of herself. Watch, she'll probably get married when I'm nine months pregnant. She'll look amazing and I'll look like a bridesmaid whale. Wait, would I be her Matron of Honor or a bridesmaid? Doesn't matter. Knowing Monica, she'll elope.

I don't want her to be right about Nadine. I'll talk to Evan about it.

Wait. I think it was my turn to pick up the bill. Crap.

Reese glanced at the time. Good thing she and Evan had no plans for the evening because it was getting late. Hopefully, he was watching football and oblivious to how late she was. Regardless, Reese called.

"Hey babe, what's up?" he answered. Reese could hear the game in the background.

"Not much, I just wanted to let you know that I'll be a little later than I thought, about another hour."

"Ok, sounds good. How was your time with Monica?"

"Good. Like always. I mean, you're the one that knows me the best but she's a close second."

"Uh-huh." Evan's voice was monotone.

Reese smiled, remembering that she was attempting conversation during a football game. "See you in an hour, handsome."

Reese hung up feeling incredibly blessed. She had a husband she loved deeply and a friend that loved her enough to risk making her uncomfortable from time to time.

Ok, so Monica heard enthusiasm in my voice. Do I really want to consider visiting these people after the campaign is over? Maybe I should give her T-Chart strategy a try. One column could say "Keep Visiting at Oak Hills" and the other side could say something like, "Let it Go." I would definitely put Rose and Dennis' names under the Keep Visiting side. Which side do I put Nadine's name on?

CHAPTER NINE

Nadine and Grandpa

"See ya in a few hours, Ree," Evan called out as he swung his bat bag on his shoulder, and grabbed his glove on the way out the door. Evan was meeting the guys for softball practice and they had planned on just throwing a pizza in the oven for dinner.

"Ok, have a great practice," she replied, eager for him to go. Reese wanted to savor the next few hours. She actually had an entire Saturday afternoon all to herself to read, an indulgence she rarely had. Two new books waited for her, still in the bag on the kitchen counter and reading would be a perfect escape from thinking about the frustrating events at work.

She poured herself a huge iced tea and put on classical music. She thought it made the perfect background sounds for reading. Across the room were their bookshelves, proudly displaying her old friends. Reese could remember when and why she acquired every one of them. She couldn't bring herself to part with a single one and Evan occasionally reminded her that their shelf realty was more than lopsided.

She got closer, and took a minute to take in every spine and title. Were there any she should really box up and donate? Her eyes rested on a book she hadn't picked up since her summers at Nadine and Grandpa's house. She was much younger then but still remembered when Nadine bought it for her in that outdated department store.

Reese pulled it off the shelf, forgetting about her new books waiting on the counter.

A piece of faded yellow paper was peeking out from the middle of the book. She opened to that page, and instantly recognized the paper. She picked it up and stared at the strong penmanship, its penciled strokes only slightly faded. *For Reese— my beautiful reader. You are my sunshine. Grandpa.* Reese got the same warm feeling reading that note all these years later, as she did the day she found it. She plopped into her favorite chair, rested the book on her knee, and stared at the timeworn note.

Growing up, she had spent a good part of her summer days at her grandparents' house. They lived in a small town about an hour away and her mom would drop her off anywhere from a few days to a couple of weeks at a time. Reese's parents worked full time, so it was helpful for them to know that she was happy and well taken care of. Since her brother was quite a bit older and already had a job during the summers, it was just Reese and her grandparents spending lazy days in the garden, or fishing in her grandpa's boat, or making crafts at the kitchen table.

Reese loved everything about those days. She would stay in their spare bedroom with the pink and white floral bedspread that Nadine, her step-grandma, bought just for her. Her bedroom window looked out over their large vegetable garden and Reese loved to survey the growth of it. She always marveled at how perfect the rows were and how her grandpa managed to keep every weed out.

He taught her all about gardening and even bought her a pair of gloves and her own kneeling pad. He showed her how to plant the seeds, when to water, weed, and when to give the plants a bit of that magic blue powder. Reese could still picture the old grey metal watering can and that dirty little plastic margarine tub that floated on top for measuring.

"Measure carefully," Grandpa always said, "plants are like people. Give 'em too much and they can't handle it."

When she and Grandpa were together, Reese usually did all the talking. Grandpa just listened and said, "I see" a lot. Reese took comfort in the fact that no matter what she talked about, even if it was something that upset her, Grandpa could be counted on to say, "I see." He never seemed to evaluate her situation or give her advice. He just faithfully listened. And it gave her comfort.

Not Nadine. Reese had an active conversation partner in her. She would ask Reese lots of questions about school, her friends, boys, or even movies. Nadine seemed to know when to ask more questions and when to let something go. She was very accepting of however Reese was feeling. Most of all, she was available. She would put down whatever she was doing and listen to Reese as if it was the most important thing in the world at that moment. Reese grew up thinking everyone was supposed to listen to her that intently. In fact, when she and Evan had one of their first arguments, she was appalled that he left the room.

Nadine married Grandpa four years after Reese's first grandmother died. Reese didn't really remember her first grandmother very well, as she was only five when she died. All she remembered was that when Nadine came into the picture, they became fast friends.

Reese liked the genuine way Nadine laughed at Grandpa's jokes, and her laughter was contagious. When he sat down at the little kitchen table for lunch, Nadine would usually come up behind him, give him a hug and whisper in his ear, "My cup overfloweth." Grandpa would smile and give Nadine's hand a squeeze. Her mom always said that Nadine was truly a godsend for Grandpa.

Saturday mornings were usually spent together at the farmer's market. Flowers, vegetables, fruits, homemade breads, crocheted dishcloths, and handmade soaps were plentiful. Reese's eyes feasted on the way each vendor displayed their goods. She loved watching the old, worn hands of the farmer's wife loading vegetables into a paper bag. Her grandparents never needed the vegetables but they always bought fresh flowers for the kitchen table.

"Reese, go ahead and pick out a bouquet you like," Nadine would say.

When they got home, it was Reese's job to cut the stems on an angle and arrange them in a vase. She got good at it over the years. To this day, when Evan brings her flowers, she takes pride in arranging them.

She loved the sight of her grandpa talking with the other retired men under the shade of a tree while waiting for Reese and Nadine. There were times that Reese wanted to sit with him to hear what old men talked about. Sports? The economy? The weather? Whatever the subject, she was sure it had to be interesting.

He always smoked a cigar while waiting for his girls under that tree. It smelled a little like vanilla. Reese marveled at how he could keep it in his mouth while talking. It bobbed up and down with each word, but never fell out. He usually tried to light it up again in the car on the rides home, but Nadine would put an end to that. "Ray, please not in the car. You know I can't stand that smell." Reese however, loved it.

Her grandparents both had a strong faith, even though they lived it out differently. Grandpa's faith was quiet. He minded his own business, helped others often, and was incredibly patient. Every morning that Reese awoke at their house, she would wander into the living room, and her first familiar sight was always Grandpa in his chair, reading the Bible.

His Bible's cover was worn and the pages flipped easily from wear. One day, when he was out cutting the grass, Reese carefully opened its cover. She wasn't sure what she was looking for, but she was certain she'd find something secretive. She didn't have to look far, as Grandpa's writing was right inside the cover. "May the words of God change the man I am." Reese remembered thinking that Grandpa was perfect just the way he was.

She noticed a bulge in the pages further down, and opened to that spot. Safely tucked between pages 914 and 915, was a picture of her family from a few years ago. His handwriting was on the back of the picture in pencil. It read, *Lord protect them and grant them faith to know you well.* Reese could hear his voice in her mind, saying those words to God and she felt so loved in that moment.

Nadine's faith was harder to see. But there was this one hymn she sang constantly when cooking or doing dishes. To this day, upon hearing an old hymn, Reese waits to see if it's Nadine's kitchen hymn. She tested herself to remember the words. *Great is thy faithfulness, oh God my Father, morning-by-morning new mercies I see, all I have needed thy hand hath provided, great is thy faithfulness, Lord unto me.* She loved the fact that Nadine sang it slightly off key.

Days at Nadine and Grandpa's always included time to do whatever you wanted. Even at a young age, reading was a passion of Reese's, so she always brought several books along to their house.

There were not one, but two magical spots to settle in and read. One was in the backyard on Nadine's hammock, if it hadn't rained the night before. It was under the big oak tree, where it got the morning sun and the afternoon shade. The other spot was in the house, upstairs in the unfinished bedroom. Reese loved it because it smelled like cedar and had exposed beams that were still in need of finished walls over them. There was a large, braided rug in the center of the wood floor and a small window, facing west. When she read in that spot after dinner, the setting sun's rays would lend their magic to whatever she was reading.

Grandpa didn't want her reading on the floor, so he had placed a small, overstuffed chair and tiny table by the window. One time when Reese went up there to read, she found a single daisy in a little vase. A note on yellow paper was propped up against the vase, the very note she now held in her hand.

She paused to sip her tea. Still holding the worn yellow note in her fingers, she decided to reflect once more on the sequence of events that altered her life. It was still so hard to forgive herself. It was not the first time that she recounted everything in an attempt to justify her actions.

She began with the day after her eighteenth birthday, the horrible day her grandpa passed away from a massive heart attack. Reese had been in shock and unable to grieve at his funeral.

As the months passed, she tried talking about it with Nadine. But Nadine had made it clear she did not want to talk about Grandpa. The third and final attempt had been the worst. They were sitting at the kitchen table, cutting up tomatoes for Nadine to can.

"Nadine, everything is so different without Grandpa. I miss him terribly, don't you?"

It seemed to Reese an honest way to bring it up, but Nadine just kept cutting tomatoes. "I don't know why I insist on canning. I swear this will be my last year."

She picked up her cutting board, took it to the sink, and turned on the garbage disposal. Reese watched as all of Nadine's perfectly cut tomatoes were scraped into the sink and shoved down the disposal. The sound was deafening and Reese froze, a lump in her throat.

Nadine turned off the disposal and the running water and grabbed the towel to wipe her hands. With her back to Reese, her shoulders drew forward, clutching the towel to her chest. She lifted it to dab each eye before turning around to face Reese.

"Honey, I know you want to talk about this, but I just can't."

Nadine's face was full of pain as she picked up the empty tomato basket and went out the back door. Reese watched her out the window as she went straight to the tomato bushes and began picking them to fill the basket once more. Reese was so confused. Anger stirred within her as she watched Nadine pick tomatoes for the garbage disposal.

She wanted so badly to follow her out to the garden and scream, "You've been my lifelong conversation partner! I'm hurting just like you! Why? Why won't you talk about Grandpa?" Canning day was the last attempt.

The summers that followed were never the same, not only because of her grandpa's death, but also because Reese now needed to work and save money during her college years. She could no longer spend days or weeks at a time at Nadine's and she missed them dearly.

One Saturday in July, after her sophomore year, Reese made it a point to take off work and spend the weekend with Nadine. They chatted until late hours at the kitchen table, eating strawberries out of the chipped green bowl. In the morning, they went to the farmer's market for the first time since Grandpa had passed. Reese's heart sank when she saw the old men under the shade of the tree, smoking their cigars.

Once they were back at the house, Reese noticed how everything seemed quieter. Grandpa used to come in from the garden, the back screen door slamming behind him. "For goodness sakes Ray, when are you going to fix that door?" Nadine would holler from the kitchen.

Before meals, Grandpa would come up behind Nadine and wrap his arms around her, whispering something in her ear that Reese could never quite make out. Nadine would giggle and sometimes dab a bit of whatever she was stirring, on his nose or cheek. Grandpa seemed to love it and his laughter would fill the kitchen. Reese was beginning to realize how the absence of one person could completely change a family's dynamics. Sights, sounds, and habits would all have to find a new comfort level.

Although that new comfort level never really arrived, the family did their best to adjust. Nadine kept busy and seemed to be living a life full of activity again. Even though Reese didn't see her as often, they still enjoyed long talks on the phone. Nadine always had an encouraging piece of advice to offer without judgment.

After Reese and Evan were engaged, Nadine faithfully listened to every one of Reese's ideas for the wedding. "Those are amazing ideas honey, but don't try too hard," Nadine would say. "People just want to witness and remember your love. The rest is soon forgotten."

And then, about six months before their wedding, Nadine was carrying a watering can to the garden, while Mr. Sanfield, the next-door neighbor happened to be taking out his garbage. He was about to call out a good morning greeting to her, when suddenly she collapsed onto the grass, still clutching her watering can. She had suffered a massive stroke.

Thankfully, Mr. Sanfield acted quickly by calling the ambulance and staying at her side, even following her to the hospital. "That Mr. Sanfield is the best kind of neighbor," Nadine used to say. Despite knowing that he had been there for her, Reese still hated the mental picture of Nadine falling to the grass. It made her slightly nauseous.

The months leading up to the wedding were incredibly stressful. Reese and her mom did their best to complete wedding tasks with some measure of joy. But there were other arrangements too, the kind that had to be made for Nadine. Her stroke left her with limitations that required daily help. Reese and her mom made phone call after phone call, checking into the availability and costs of home care. Somehow, those calls drained the excitement from everything else.

It became harder to concentrate and keep the wedding details separate from the rest. Reese remembered one call in particular.

"Thank you for calling Flannery's Catering, how may I help you?"

"Yes, how much do you charge for installing handicapped railings in a bathroom?"

"I'm sorry ma'am, I think you have the wrong number."

"Wait, I'm sorry. I meant to ask, how much do you charge per plate for the Polynesian wedding buffet?"

Even the hour drive to Nadine's house that used to be relaxing, was now draining. It was a chore to fit in quick visits to check in on her. Reese's new position at work was challenging as well, and she felt like maybe she jumped in over her head. Her boss assured her that it would just take more time to learn the job. *Yeah, time I don't have,* she thought.

In spite of everything, she and Evan managed to pull off the wedding with most of her wishes intact. Yet, on that day, not even her carefully chosen bouquet seemed to matter much anymore. All that mattered to Reese was the assurance of seeing two faces, Evan's waiting for her at the front of the church, and Nadine's sitting at the end of the pew in her wheelchair.

Reese wasn't even discouraged by the fact that Nadine was in a wheelchair or that she couldn't eat the reception food. It didn't matter that she would need to be taken home early in the evening when she tired. All that mattered to Reese was that she was there. Complete with corsage and loving smile on her face– *she was there.* Reese glanced up at the wedding picture of her and Evan with Nadine, now beautifully framed and hanging on their living room wall.

It wasn't long after they were married, that Nadine needed even more care and was admitted to the nursing home that Reese's mom and uncle had chosen. It was lovely but on the expensive side. Worst of all, it was almost a three-hour drive. *Three hours.* Reese's uncle wanted to split the distance between them, so that his family could see her more often as well.

At first, Reese figured that she and Evan could make the trip once a month. That seemed reasonable. Evan agreed that he would go with her and they could use the driving time for long talks. And they did. Twice. And then winter hit, and the weather always seemed miserable when they had plans to go. With either the snow or ice-covered roads, driving would be unsafe or taxing at best. Reese told herself they would make up for it during the spring when the roads were clear. Phone calls would have to do for now.

However, early that March she was promoted and the new expectations of her job caught up with her. Reese's hours were long and she needed to bring work home almost every night. She and Evan were finding it hard to spend any time together, leading to more arguments.

I can't take off this Saturday to drive up there, when I haven't had any time with my husband for weeks. I already feel distant from him and I know Nadine wouldn't want that.

Two more months passed with no visit. One April evening, while she was loading the dishwasher after a late dinner with Evan, her phone rang. Evan answered it and then held it to his chest while he whispered to Reese, "It's your mom. She sounds like she's been crying."

Reese took the phone, her heart beating a little faster. "Mom, what's going on?"

"Oh honey, I'm so sorry to have to tell you this."

Reese's mind raced while her mom cried and finally said, "Nadine passed away tonight. The aide walked into her room to help get her ready for bed, and found her sitting in her chair, with her chin to her chest. He thought she was just sleeping, but...."

Reese no longer heard her mom's words. The room was blurry and it was hard to breathe. The grief came quickly, like when a storm begins with a pounding rain. Reese slowly sank to the kitchen floor, crying with her hand over her mouth.

She kept her phone next to her ear, hearing her mother's voice but not knowing what she was saying. And then, without even realizing it, she laid the phone down on the open door of the dishwasher, as her tears gave way to heaving sobs.

Evan picked it up and talked with her mom for a few minutes. "Kate? It's me. I'm so sorry to hear about Nadine. Yeah, I will. Absolutely. I'm so sorry, Kate. Yes, we'll call you first thing in the morning."

Reese was depressed the first few months and spent a lot of time on the phone with her mom, as if it would make up for the time missed with Nadine. Eventually, life got back to normal, but a newfound guilt made its home in Reese's heart. She made frequent trips to the cemetery, and was incredibly upset if she and Evan had to miss a family birthday or holiday.

The following summer, she and Evan decided to go to an outdoor jazz concert. They brought a picnic supper and were relaxing on a blanket, eating sandwiches and talking. An elderly couple walked past and set up their lawn chairs nearby.

Reese stared at them, and then looked back at Evan with a smile on her face. "Aren't they cute?" she said. "That's us in fifty years, babe."

Evan had wanted to say something to her for a long time and this moment seemed perfect. "Hey, Ree, remember what a great listener Nadine was?"

"Of course I do."

He paused and then carefully continued. "Well, I want you to know that you're a great listener, too. You picked that up from her, I think."

Reese smiled and popped another grape in her mouth. "You think so? Even those times when I dominate the conversation?"

He laughed, "Well, maybe not those times. But, really. I was thinking…what if you were to listen to others who need it?"

"Sorry babe, not following you."

"It's just that, I think you would be great at listening to old people. You and Nadine had such a cool relationship and she modeled how to listen. What if you were to do something like that for someone else?"

"The ol' pay it forward thing, huh?"

"Yeah, I guess."

Reese looked back at the elderly couple, now holding hands in their lawn chairs. Maybe they had been coming for years. Reese tried to imagine what they might have looked like in their twenties. She could picture herself sitting across from one of their weathered faces, listening to a long-forgotten story, perhaps over a bowl of strawberries.

Hearing a slow song begin, Reese stood up and held her

hand out to Evan. "Dance with me?"

Evan looked around, shrugged and stood up to join her. He pulled her close with his hand on the small of her back; the spot that always made her feel safe.

As they swayed to the soothing notes of the saxophone, Reese looked up at Evan.

His blue eyes were still intoxicating and so were his words. *What if you were to listen to others who need it?*

How ironic. It was almost two years ago now that they had danced to the saxophone. On that night, Evan's suggestion had intrigued her. He made it sound so romantic, like a compassionate linking of the generations. Yet on that night, his suggestion floated by like the notes of the music.

Reese slipped her grandpa's note back in the book and took in a deep breath, letting the air out slowly.

And now here I am, years later, listening to others who need it. It's incredible how it all happened, as if being a visitor was a destined part of my path. What would Nadine think of my role at Oak Hills? Nadine...the one who went for months and months without a visit from me, without even a good bye.

CHAPTER TEN

Earl

"You're back!" Rose seemed delighted and Reese was instantly glad she came, her nagging guilt about Nadine melting quickly.

"Hi Rose. I was hoping you'd have time for a visit today." Reese never felt as if she was intruding upon Rose.

"Are you kiddin' me? I'd love it." Rose eagerly rose from her chair and grabbed her nearby walker, already out of breath from the effort. "Here honey, sit here," Rose offered the only chair in her room and began making her way to the bed.

After all this time making visits, Reese had learned that residents still wanted something to offer their guests, even if it was just a chair to sit in. "Thank you, Rose."

"So tell me, how are things going at your job? Any jerks bothering you?"

Reese laughed. *Please, let me be like her when I'm old.* "No, no jerks. The people are pretty great and I still love my work. I'm lucky."

"I should say you are. And I'm glad you realize it. Grateful hearts are hard to come by."

Reese smiled. "Mmm. I suppose so. How have you been,

Rose? Are you feeling ok?"

"Well honey, I tell you what. I don't like people who complain. And I sure as hell don't want to be one of 'em. Is this where I saw myself living in my 80's? No. But it's the best we can do for now. And I'm just glad there are folks who want these jobs. Would *you* want to help old people on and off the toilet? I know I wouldn't."

"No, I wouldn't. Definitely something to be thankful for."

Rose had on a baseball jersey, as always, but this one had a stain that resembled gravy near the top button. Apparently, Rose was aware of it too. "Honey, would you do me a big favor? Would you go to my closet and bring me a clean jersey?"

"Sure," Reese was already on her feet and headed to the closet with the sliding door. As she pushed the door back, she was surprised at just how small Rose's closet space was. Jackets, pants, tops, nightgowns, were all scrunched on a single rack separated by a hollow piece of wood for the other resident's belongings. Reese instantly thought of her own closet, easily five times the size.

"Which one would you like, Rose?"

"Is the Marlins jersey clean? That one looks good on me."

Reese smiled at Rose's relentless positive spin and set out to find the Marlins. There was barely enough room on the rack to separate clothes. Reese was relieved to find the right one. "Yup, here it is. You're right, Rose, this is a cool one."

Reese brought the jersey to Rose, still on the hanger, and laid it next to her on the bed.

Rose began unbuttoning the jersey with the stain, her crippled hands fumbling with each button, testing Reese's patience. She desperately wanted to jump in and help Rose, but she wasn't family and it seemed way too awkward. "Should I get an aide for you?"

"No, I can do it." More waiting. Reese took in a deep breath. *Just give it a minute. She probably wants the dignity of being able to change her own shirt.*

Now down to the last button, Rose looked up at Reese with a sad, defeated face, one Reese had not seen until now. "I'm sorry, but would you mind helping me get the clean one on?"

"Of course not." Reese tried to act as if this was a typical request and no big deal. She gingerly lifted Rose's arm up and out of the first sleeve, then the second. Seeing Rose sitting on the bed in her bra with her wrinkled exposed skin lying in layers, stirred a protective response in Reese. Looking over her shoulder, she made sure Rose's door was closed, and then began nervously chatting in an effort to make Rose feel comfortable while she dressed her in the clean jersey.

"Would you like to do the buttons Rose or should I?"

"You can, if that's alright." Rose kept her eyes down, looking at her recent manicure. "There's a lady who comes once a week and gives us manicures. I knew this would be a good red."

Reese was relieved that Rose had changed the subject for

them both; she finished buttoning the Marlins jersey. "You're right, that is a perfect red. It will go with a lot of things."

She sat back down in the chair as quickly as she could, hoping Rose would not feel too embarrassed having been dressed by her.

"You want to know why I really wear baseball jerseys?" Rose was leaning towards Reese, as if about to welcome her into a secret.

Reese nodded and smiled at Rose.

"Well, I hate old lady clothes. That's one reason." Reese laughed, loving Rose's attitude.

"You see baseball is a non-violent sport. It brings people together and helps them forget their problems for a while. My stepfather's name was Earl and he was a violent man. Growing up, he'd hit my mother from time to time and I was always afraid he'd hit me, too. Instead, he'd yell and break things in the house when he got mad at me. The only time I wasn't afraid of him was when he watched baseball. He often watched on television and it seemed to soothe him. He'd teach me things about the game while it was on. 'See how that shortstop dove for the ball, Rose? His throw didn't get that runner out, but his belly is covered with dirt from tryin'. That's what real effort is all about.'"

Rose's face looked peaceful, despite all she must have endured. "He was a hard worker. But I was determined never to marry someone like him. And so, my first husband was kind, quiet and didn't say much. I guess we both had scars that we hadn't figured out yet." Rose shrugged and looked down at her jersey, passing her fingers over the embroidered team logo.

"So, wearing baseball jerseys...?" Reese let her voice trail off hoping Rose would finish the sentence. Rose was quiet for a moment, looking off to the corner of the room collecting her thoughts.

"I think the jerseys remind me that there's always a bright spot, even in the dark times. Baseball was my saving grace as a child and to this day when I watch a game, I feel safe." She looked into Reese's eyes, as if waiting for a reply.

"That's a good reason, Rose." Reese instantly decided Rose's stepfather was to be hated. But what she hated more was the thought that this wonderful woman still had haunting memories, even into old age.

"Rose, this is none of my business so you certainly don't have to answer this, but did you hate him? Your stepfather, I mean."

"Oh, there were moments I hated him. But there were also moments I saw good in him. He never turned down a neighbor or friend who asked for help of any kind. He taught me a lot about baseball, and even how to change a tire on a car. And whenever he saw me working on a school project at the kitchen table, he would sit down and help."

Reese thought of her own father. *He would never hit Mom in a million years.*

"You know Reese, people who hurt other people are usually

all bottled up with their own hurts and fears. Took me a long time to understand that. My mother should've left him, but for whatever reason, she didn't. I had to work at it, but I finally found peace."

"Meaning…you forgave him?"

Rose sighed a heavy sigh that seemed to come from strength rather than sorrow.

"I suppose I did. It would have been a lot more work to hate him."

"So then, why do you still need baseball to feel safe?"

"Oh honey, I didn't say I *needed* it to feel safe. It just reminds me that there's good and bad in everyone."

Yeah Rose, but some people's bad is far worse than other people's bad. Has she minimized that he hit her mother?

Apparently, Rose read the disapproval on Reese's face. "It can take a long time before the dust settles in our hearts. Took me about 25 years."

Reese was quiet, trying to sort through Rose's story. "By 'dust settling', you mean…"

Rose's answer came quickly, as if she had been waiting to explain it to someone her entire life. "You gotta talk to someone. Find a good church. Read what the good Lord says about life. Find a friend or counselor who helps you sort it out. Folks just keep tryin' to do it all themselves and I'm here to tell you, it doesn't work. My first marriage and years of tryin' to please people are proof of that."

Reese loved the passion in Rose's voice and how open she was about her life. And she especially loved the purity of her intentions to save Reese from future pain.

Reese nodded her head. "Sounds like good advice, Rose. Thank you for sharing all of that with me."

"Honey, trust me. Life has a way of catching up with all of us. When it does, just remember one thing—don't try to figure it out on your own, get help." Rose was leaning forward now, tears in her eyes.

"I'll remember Rose. I promise."

Reese used the drive home to play Rose's story over in her head. She tried to picture what Earl had looked like. Was he a big man, whose blows took weeks to recover from? Were his sleeves always rolled up from work? Did he hate himself for hitting Rose's mother or feel justified in doing it? Why did she stay with him? Were there really no other options?

Reese believed in forgiveness but Rose's story made her doubt that belief. *If I were Rose, could I forgive Earl?* Reese felt sure that there must be reasonable boundaries for forgiveness. After all, how could anyone forgive something like rape or murder? Or even the injustices done in the privacy of homes?

She pulled into her apartment parking lot. Reese sat for a minute before going inside, burdened that she no longer had forgiveness figured out. Like every other time she needed to reflect, she pulled out her iPad and began typing.

Visited Rose today. She shared why she wears baseball jerseys and her story shook my understanding of forgiveness. How is it possible for anyone to forgive someone who has deeply hurt them? Hurt feelings, sure, but violence? Maybe if justice is served first, forgiveness might follow. But honestly, I don't know if I could forgive my Dad if he hit my Mom. I'd like to think I could. Oh Rose, how did you do it? How did you forgive Earl?

Forgiveness. Reese stared at the word. It looked daunting, even mysterious…yet, strangely inviting.

CHAPTER ELEVEN

Skip

By the sixth month of volunteering at Oak Hills, Kelly was highlighting more names on the list than Reese could count. And work at the agency was piling up. She couldn't afford to let the hour get too long before getting back to her office. *I refuse to be overwhelmed. Even if I only visit one, it'll make a difference.* She quickly decided to start with Charles, a rather new resident who always looked sad. Reese had only visited with him once before and she recalled it had been fairly pleasant.

Charles was in his room watching TV when Reese knocked on his door. He was alert and layered with a warm cardigan and blankets bundled over his legs. Reese never assumed that a resident would remember her, especially if she had only met him once. So many of them struggled with some form of dementia or at least the challenges of old age. She would need to begin again with introductions just in case.

"Hi Charles, I'm Reese. I volunteer here."

Sure enough, he did not remember her. "Hello, nice to meet you. People call me Skip. "

"Alright, Skip." Reese asked permission to sit on his bed,

as there were no chairs for visitors. Skip shrugged and so she moved his morning paper and sat down. He asked her to hand him the remote so that he could turn off the TV. Reese wished he would leave it on, as it sometimes proved a helpful distraction.

They made introductory small talk and Skip mentioned that he had a daughter who looked like her. Reese estimated his age at 80-85, so maybe he meant a granddaughter?

"I haven't seen her in years. She won't talk to me. She doesn't even know I'm here."

Disclosures like this had to be taken with a grain of salt. How much was imagined? How much was old information that had long since changed but wasn't remembered? And worse yet, how much was actually the truth?

"I'm sorry to hear that Skip." Reese tried to change the subject. "Did you grow up in this town?"

"No, I'm from the Bronx. I lived there with my mother. My Dad died when I was a kid and then at 18, I told my mother that I wanted to go into the Army. She wasn't happy, but I did it anyway."

Reese was always amazed at how open most of the residents were with their private life details. Often times they would spill out confidences as if talking about the weather. Maybe it was because they were aware of how few years they had left. Or maybe the need for privacy no longer seemed necessary.

"What did you do in the Army?" Military conversations

were always tricky for Reese. She wanted to show interest and yet, never quite knew what she was getting herself into.

"I was a paratrooper during the Korean War. I jumped for three years."

Reese was afraid of heights and couldn't begin to imagine jumping out of a plane. "Wow, Skip, that's impressive. Thank you for serving our country in that way."

Thanking veterans early on in a conversation was something Nadine had taught her. "It may feel awkward at first, but you'll be glad you did," she'd advise. Whenever she was with Nadine and they'd see a serviceman in uniform, Nadine nudged. Reese obliged and always received a big smile and a "thank you" in return.

With her appreciation declared, Reese figured they would move on to another subject, never anticipating Skip's next words. "I can't get the picture out of my head," he said with his voice already breaking. "Did you know that when a guy's chute fails to open, his body actually bounces when he hits the ground? I jumped right next to my buddy and his chute didn't open."

Skip was so choked up now he could barely continue. "I saw his body hit the ground and bounce back into the air." He began to sob into his handkerchief. Reese just waited. Skip cleared his throat several times. "It's the worst thing ever."

Reese had no idea what to say. She just sat there on the bed and didn't move a muscle.

"You give your life to the Army and what do you get for it? My knee was crushed on a jump and they couldn't fix it. My other buddies were killed on a mission I should've been on, but because of my knee, they sent me home. I shouldn't even be here and now look at me. I can't walk, I got no money, my kids don't even talk to me!"

"I'm so sorry, Skip," was all Reese could say. He kept going.

"I hated being home. So I was a gambler, a drinker, and a womanizer. No wonder my wife left me. I owe my kids money and I want to pay them back, but just look at me—how am I supposed to do that? I can't do nothin'!"

Skip was obviously dealing with a lot. Reese was all too aware of the fact that she couldn't even remotely relate to his situation. What could she possibly say that would bring him any comfort? That feeling of inadequacy that sometimes surfaced during difficult visits, taunted her to make up a reason to leave.

You're in over your head. Just tell him you have to go, he'll probably forget you in five minutes anyway.

But both pity and gratitude for his service kept her firmly in place on his bed. Reese knew nothing of military sacrifice but she did understand pain. So she sat with him quietly.

A tender impulse overcame her and she watched powerlessly as her own hand reached over and took his large, wrinkled hand in hers. She cradled it like a treasure, her right hand underneath and her left hand on the top. She said nothing, and kept her eyes on their joined hands. His hand was large and feeble and she wondered why it was cold, even though he was layered with blankets. A silence followed that Reese was surprisingly comfortable with. It may have been seconds or even several minutes, she wasn't sure.

"You're a nice lady," he said softly.

Reese wondered how young Skip's hands looked when his father died? How strong were they when he jumped out of Army airplanes? How steady were they when he held drink after drink at the casinos? How long were they cupped over his face to hide his tears in the wake of divorce and estrangement from his kids? How she wished it had been different for him.

"Would it be okay if I visited you again, Skip?"

He nodded. "I would like that."

Reese lifted her top hand off his and gently patted it. Slowly, she withdrew her other hand, as if trying not to wake a baby.

"Shall I turn the TV back on?" She offered.

"Yeah, sure."

"There you go. I'll see you again, Skip." Reese left slowly, almost reverently, not wanting him to feel abandoned.

Once on the other side of his door, she let out a heavy sigh and turned to look back into Skip's room. He looked identical to how she found him when she first came in, almost as if her visit had never occurred. *Will our time together matter to him later? Will he remember?*

Reese found an empty chair at the end of the hallway and dutifully sat down to record her visit. She kept her comments in the volunteer file benign, not wanting to expose the moment they had.

Reese debated writing anything at all in her personal notes. She was surprised to have felt a connection with Skip, someone she didn't understand. Yet she couldn't help but want a better life for him and so she typed.

For the first time, I had the privilege of hearing a veteran's story and his pain bled far beyond the years he spent in Korea. The price for serving our country sometimes seems too high. Did Skip choose drinking and gambling or did the haunts of war choose it for him?

CHAPTER TWELVE

Evan

As Reese drove to Oak Hills, the calendar was on her mind. Had she really been volunteering for almost a year? The Adopt a Neighbor campaign ended five months ago. Caprice was surprised that Reese kept visiting in her free time. "You've got to get a life, girl!"

Mike however, would ask about the residents from time to time. "So how's the veteran? And how's the lady who reminds you of your grandma? You know Reese, I had a feeling you'd like this if you just gave it a shot." Mike loved being right. But even more, he loved it when his employees were engaged with the community.

What Mike and Caprice didn't know, was that Reese had become incredibly fond of a few of the residents, especially Rose. Rose was now a sort of mentor to Reese. She couldn't wait to hear what would come out of Rose's mouth next, knowing it would either make her laugh or make her think. Reese was headed there now, purposely waiting until after work, so that her time with Rose would not be cut short.

As she entered the atrium, the beauty of the last rays of

today's sun stunned her. They streaked across the lobby carpeting and cast a gentle welcome to the early evening.

"Hey, can you take me outside? No one around here will take me outside."

It was Vincent sitting in the far corner of the atrium, keeping watch for any able-bodied person who would oblige his request. He usually yelled in the hallways and loudly made his requests known in public.

Reese sighed. She didn't want to stop for Vincent this time, but she knew that he loved the outdoors and that most employees tired quickly of his badgering. "Just a minute Vincent. Let me check with the desk."

He was cleared for sitting outside, so Reese pushed him out into the gardens to a lovely spot by all of the birdfeeders. "Oh, this is nice. You gonna sit with me now, right?"

"I can't right now. Maybe later, ok? Besides, it'll get dark soon, Vincent."

Reese reminded the front desk that someone would need to bring him back in fairly soon. She hurried to Rose's room and knocked on the door. Peeking around the edge, she hoped to catch Rose's eye and see the smile her visit would bring.

"She's gone," blurted Rose's roommate. Reese was confused and looked carefully around the room. Rose's bed was bare—no bedspread, no pillow. The top of her dresser was cleared off and the corner chair that Rose always draped her blanket over was empty. No pink blanket.

"Well, where is she?" asked Reese.

"She's gone," shrugged the roommate. "Will you tell them to let me keep the room to myself?"

Ignoring Little Miss Sunshine, Reese turned on her heel and hurried back down the hall to the nurse's station. Only one nurse was there and she was on the phone. *Where on earth did they move her?* Reese was getting nervous. She waited for several minutes. *Did this nurse even see her waiting there? Why had they moved Rose?*

She had been patient long enough. Reese grabbed the edge of the countertop with both hands and leaned forward. "Excuse me. I just need a question answered," her voice dripping with annoyance.

"Can you hold on a minute?" the nurse asked the person on the phone and put the receiver on her shoulder, raising her eyebrows at Reese. "Yes?"

"I just went in to visit Rose Renquist and her stuff is gone. When was she moved?"

"Can I take your number and call you back please?" the nurse asked her caller. Finally giving her attention to Reese, she asked, "Are you family?"

"No, but I visit Rose often. She's a good friend."

"Mmm. Well, I'm sorry to have to tell you this, but Rose died last Thursday."

Reese froze. She stared at the nurse; her throat felt instantly dry. She felt her stomach tighten and her hands begin to tremor. *Who was this nurse and could she be right? And how could she announce Rose's death so bluntly?*

Hot tears were filling her eyes and she was unable to speak. She wanted to run back to Rose's room to see if it was all a cruel joke. Maybe this time, Rose would be there. *Rose died last Thursday...*Reese backed away from the nurse's station, while staring at the nurse.

"Miss? Miss, I'm sorry. We all loved Rose. She died in her sleep and..."

Reese didn't even hear the nurse explaining the details. She had to have air. She had to call Evan. In a daze, she began walking down the hallway toward the atrium. *Rose died last Thursday.* She walked faster now, wanting only to get out.

As the front doors opened widely, Reese bolted into a full run. She held her purse tightly to her chest, her head pounding each time her feet hit the pavement. The vast gardens on her left were merely a blur. Vincent saw her running past and he called out to her at the top of his voice. "Reese! Hey Reese! You gonna visit me?"

Where was her car? *Rose died last Thursday...*There it was in the last row of the lot. She reached it out of breath and fumbled in her bag for the keys. She got in, slammed the door, and started the engine. Without even checking her mirrors, she put it in reverse and backed out.

She sped out of the parking lot then slammed on the brakes for a red light. She noticed a Target store was across the street and a large part of their lot was empty. It seemed a private place to stop. Her head was pounding. When the light turned green, Reese sped through the intersection and pulled into the lot. She shifted into park, shut her car off, and looked around to make sure no one could see her.

Rose died last Thursday...

With lower lip quivering and hands shaking, Reese let the pain come. She cried until she was so congested she had to stop and blow her nose. *Why didn't I go last week? I could have seen her before she died! Oh, Rose. Why didn't I go?*

And then it dawned on her. The funeral. There would be a funeral. Was it possible it hadn't taken place yet? She frantically pulled her phone from her purse, her hands still shaking while typing Rose's name. After a quick search, she found the obituary online. Swiping down, Reese frantically looked for a date, a time. *Wait, yes...there it is...what?...yesterday? The funeral service was yesterday?* She stared at the funeral details on the screen until her phone went dark.

She missed it. She missed Rose's funeral. Reese sat motionless, staring out her windshield, feeling exhausted and defeated. *Rose is dead.* Reese sat stunned, her nose now dripping into her mouth, her head still throbbing. She reached for a tissue and hung her head to relieve the stress building in her neck. Looking down at her chest, Reese saw the volunteer badge still around her neck. She took it off and held it in her hand, staring at the nursing home logo above her name.

Anger rose from her heart up into her face, and she accusingly spoke to that little logo on her badge. "What makes you think I want to come there anymore?" It felt good to place blame and she yelled all the louder. "Well, I don't! If you think I'm coming back for more of this, you're screwed, cause I'm *not!*" She threw her badge on the passenger floorboard and started the car. Anger seemed to fill her body like adrenaline and she welcomed it, gripping the wheel tightly.

She drove home way too fast, screaming out loud in the car the entire time. "I don't care, you hear me? I don't care! I don't need this! Don't need it. Don't you think I have other things to do? Don't you think there are a *million* other things I could be doing? Well, there are! A million!" It felt good to scream. It felt good to drive too fast, as if driving recklessly could absorb her pain.

When her car entered their neighborhood, Reese finally slowed down. She pulled into their apartment lot, and turned off the engine. Her body went numb and heavy and she had no ambition to get out of the car. Exhausted, Reese leaned back in her seat and closed her eyes. Her face felt hot and she wore her headache like a helmet.

She tried to see Rose and replay their last conversation in her mind. What had they talked about? Oh, yes. She could see Rose's face now, from the side, staring out her window, looking unusually sad. It was the last time they spoke and Reese had asked her how she handled the passing of her second husband, her soul mate.

"How did you do it, Rose? How did you ever manage after he died?"

Rose seemed to wait a very long time before answering Reese. Her gaze fixed out the window, she answered so softly that Reese could barely hear her. "You learn to live with the ache."

Learn to live with the ache. Reese couldn't think about the future right now. It was all she could do to get out of the car and go into the apartment. Three ibuprofen and a glass of wine later, Reese was sound asleep on the bed.

In the weeks that followed, Reese found reasons why she couldn't make visits. She didn't even respond to the email from Kelly, the Volunteer Director, asking how she was doing and expressing how they missed her.

One night towards the end of their dinner, Evan brought it up. "Reese, it's been a long time since you've been to the House of Fun."

"Yeah I know. I've had too much going on. I can't keep going there Evan and they shouldn't expect me to."

Evan refilled their wine glasses. Taking a sip, he looked at her over the rim. "Hey babe, is everything okay?"

"Yeah, of course," she answered. "Why?"

Evan continued to study her face. "Well, it's just not like you to avoid a challenge."

Reese loved how Evan knew her so well. But sometimes, when she wanted to hide her emotions, she wished he wasn't so observant. "It's just hard, you know?" she began. "You know how special Rose was to me, and I don't want to see someone else in her room."

Evan was quiet and sat back from the table. He kept his eyes on Reese and just waited for her to continue. *How did he know when there was more?*

Reese looked away, toward the living room. She knew Evan would wait as long as it took for her to speak. He was never in a hurry with a conversation. It was one of things she decided was rare in a man. The only other man that gave her all the space she needed to express her feelings was Grandpa.

She pictured the hallways, rooms, and faces that had made up such a big part of her weekly world. "There are only a few that I really got attached to" Reese hesitated, "and it hurts when they're gone. Well, it hurts now that *she's* gone."

She had pushed back any thoughts of Rose for the last four weeks but now she could see her clearly, her face lighting up when Reese would walk in the room. She tried to recreate Rose's voice in her mind, but without success. Reese desperately wanted her back. She needed her stories and her gentle lessons on life. She needed her to be permanent.

Reese used the edge of her napkin to absorb the tears welling in her eyes and then looked back at Evan. He had the kindest look on his face.

"Babe…I know you loved Rose. But I think you have to ask yourself something. Can you accept that there might be more goodbyes than hellos?"

She knew it was true. After all, Rose wasn't the first goodbye Reese had experienced. It's just that her death came unexpectedly and Reese hadn't time to mentally prepare.

"Yes, I can, if I have time to prepare for them," she answered.

Evan reached for her hand and asked softly, "What makes you think we're owed time to prepare?"

He gave her hand a gentle squeeze, stood up, and gathered their plates and forks. After stacking their dishes in the sink, he headed up the stairs, leaving her with her thoughts.

Reese sat for a long time at the kitchen table.

More goodbyes than hellos…is that why I don't want to go back? Am I too afraid that someone else I care about will die unexpectedly…again?

Determined to figure it out, Reese brought her iPad to bed with the intent of journaling. Maybe her written words would reveal something she hadn't acknowledged. She was getting too sleepy to filter her thoughts and her fingers typed the raw emotion swirling in her head. *Rose is dead. No more visits with her. No more laughs with her. No more timely advice. Just like… just like Nadine.*

Reese lifted her eyes off the words and onto Max, lying at the foot of their bed. He let out a sigh and looked back at her with his faithful black eyes. The last thing Reese wanted to do in that moment was grieve Nadine. She was too tired, too afraid of the similarities.

I just need a change, she reasoned. Reese decided to search online for new volunteer possibilities. *I have tomorrow off. I'm sure to find something that interests me.* Evan was reading and ready to turn out the lights. She laid the iPad on the floor, pulled the covers up and got comfortable on his chest.

"Am I making too big a deal out of this?" she asked Evan in the dark.

"I don't know, Ree. But usually when we avoid something, it's best to figure out why."

Reese's eyes were heavy and she yawned a response. "Mmm." The last thing she was conscious of were Evan's fingers running through her hair.

In the morning, she felt much better. The heaviness in her chest was gone. She could now linger over her coffee and play with Max. Sunshine streamed through the patio door, and she felt a surge of confidence. Taking Max's furry snout in both her hands, she asked him, "And what say you, my friend? Any comment?" Max licked her hand and then her face with his usual gratitude for attention.

Reese got up from the floor and bolted up the stairs, two at a time, Max at her heels. As she got ready, it surprised her just how easy it was to decide to go back. For whatever reason, the morning had arrived bearing a fresh perspective.

As she got ready, her mind was taking inventory of the names and faces of those she had not visited in almost a month. *Have any of them forgotten me? Will there be someone new in Rose's room?*

Reese finished putting on her makeup and looked at herself in the mirror. The young woman staring back at her looked stronger than the one who spoke doubts in her mind. She was about to find out if she could recover from deep disappointment by facing it head on. *This time, the visits are for me.*

CHAPTER THIRTEEN

Hank

"Welcome back, stranger." It was Kelly. She happened to be behind the front desk when Reese first returned. "How are you? We were all hoping nothing went wrong in your world."

Reese knew Kelly was sincere, but didn't want to explain. "Oh, I'm great. Fine, really. Just a crazy month, that's all. Sorry I never got back to your email."

"Oh, I understand how life can get sometimes. Actually, I'm so glad to see you here today, because there's a resident that could really use your company."

"Okay. No problem. I'll start there."

Kelly explained that Hank Thompson would be transitioning soon to hospice. Of course, Reese knew that meant he was terminal with little time left. She had never visited with a hospice patient before. *What am I supposed to say to someone who knows that he's dying?*

Reese's stomach fluttered and her arms had that weak feeling she got every time her nerves took over. Evan's words the other night flashed through her mind. *It's not like you to avoid a challenge.* "Sure Kelly, I'll visit him."

Reese found Hank's room and hesitated outside his door. It usually took some measure of courage to knock on a new door and visit a new face. But this might be their only visit together. *What in the world am I going to say? He knows he's dying.* Reese drew in a deep breath and decided to get it over with.

She knocked firmly but didn't wait for a response before walking in. Reese hoped to find him sleeping so that she could justify turning around and leaving. Instead, she found Hank wide-awake in his wheelchair, the room eerily quiet.

"Good morning, Hank. My name is Reese. Nice to meet you."

Reese held out her hand and Hank shook it weakly. She was taken back at how big he was. Broad shoulders, large hands, long arms. If he stood up from his wheelchair, Reese predicted he would be tall enough to duck in doorways.

"Hank, I'm a volunteer here, and I just wanted to introduce myself and say that I'm sorry to hear you're having a tough time."

Hank looked down in his lap and spoke without looking at her. "Yeah, you could say that," he said.

Then silence. Followed by more silence. *Okay, this is going to be really difficult.*

"May I sit down?" Reese asked pulling a nearby chair in front of him.

He nodded and avoided looking at her.

"So, I understand that you've got a lot going on right now?" Reese tried to state the obvious in a subtle way to get the conversation going.

"Things are changing," he said softly.

Reese wanted her every word to be compassionate. "I see."

He fixed his eyes on something across the room. "I'm here and my wife is at home. I worry about her."

Reese could easily imagine this big guy looking after his wife. She felt sorry for him.

"I told them I don't want these blood transfusions anymore. I just want to go home and see my wife."

"Of course." She said quietly. More silence.

"I never thought that when we bought our house it would be too small. This wheelchair doesn't get around there so good."

Reese tried to affirm him, "Yes, that would be hard to predict."

Silence again. Reese looked around the room. There wasn't a single thing from home. Nothing. The room was sterile and looked as if the next person could move right in.

Only the blanket across his legs looked like it was from home.

"I used to play baseball. I was scouted for a while. But… things didn't work out."

Hank's focus was back down in his lap. He still had not looked at her.

"I love baseball. What position did you play?"

"First base. I was tall. Not a lot got past me."

Reese smiled, "I'll bet not."

Hank took a deep breath and sighed. He appeared incredibly

weak. Reese wondered if the reason Hank was so slow when talking was because it took too much energy.

"We went to the championship two years in a row. But I don't want to talk about that."

"Okay," Reese said as she wondered why he didn't want to talk about a championship. Even at his age, Reese could tell that he had been an athlete. It made sense now. The big hands, the broad but humped shoulders, the tall frame that was cramped in that wheelchair. She could imagine him at first base, stretching long for the out.

"What's your wife's name?"

Hank looked at Reese for the first time. His eyes were a beautiful light blue and she could see that his face had been handsome at one time. "Olivia. Olivia Thompson. She's Danish… and stubborn."

Reese laughed out loud, a laugh that burst into the room perhaps a bit too much. "I know what you mean," she said, "my husband's grandma is Danish and stubborn, too." Reese was encouraged that they were connecting. "Tell me about Olivia. Is she well?"

Hank stared straight ahead this time. "Our daughter looks in on her. She brings her here when she can." He wiped his eye and looked back down in his lap.

Reese thought to herself, *better not push it. He seems so tired.* And then Hank took a very deep breath as if to prepare for more talking.

"I went to church all my life. Always did believe in God. That's where I met Olivia. We've been married for sixty-eight years."

"Sixty-eight years? Wow, that's wonderful." Reese tried to sound upbeat.

It was hard to gauge Hank. The strong, silent type for sure. His voice was deep, but soft. His breathing was labored. *Did he want her to stay or go?* Another deep breath. "I've tried to treat everybody the same, like they were from Hollywood."

Reese was intrigued by the novelty of his words. *Like they were from Hollywood.* It was then, that Hank looked directly into her eyes for a second time.

"It's not right to treat people different. We're all the same," he said.

At that moment, Reese understood what he was doing. He was taking inventory of his life...his accomplishments, his marriage, how he treated others. And she was privy to it.

More silence, but this time it felt more like rest.

Reese had never been in a visit like this one. She usually felt like she had control. But Hank was different. Even though it took effort for him to talk, he was definitely the one in control. Reese had instant respect for him.

"They'll be coming soon to take me for my transfusion. I hate those things."

Reese couldn't imagine lying in a hospital bed while they change out all of your blood.

"I think I'd hate them, too," she said.

"I don't want many more. If I had known our house would be too small…" his voice trailed off, "well, not much can be done about that now."

Reese realized that not being home with his wife was what mattered most to him.

She tried to sound reassuring. "I'm sure your daughter is doing a good job looking after your wife."

"When I go to bed at night, I always wonder. Will this be the last one? Will she be ok?"

Reese's eyes filled with tears. There was no way she wanted to cry in front of him. He was staring death straight in the eye and not flinching. The least she could do was try to be as strong as him. She swallowed, and now she was the one to look into her lap. "Hank, I'm sure Olivia will be okay."

An aide with dark skin and tender brown eyes, walked into the room and stood in front of Hank. "Mr. Thompson? The shuttle is here. We're going to get you ready to go for your transfusion now."

Hank didn't reply to her. He gave Reese one more glance. "The next time you come, I might be gone."

She knew exactly what he meant. Two tears streamed down her face and this time, she couldn't stop them. Reese decided not to wipe them away. Instead, she smiled and looked into those weary blue eyes.

"If you're not here when I come back," she said, "I'll know you beat me to home base."

Hank nodded slightly and put his head back down.

The aide wrapped another blanket around his shoulders, and stood behind his wheelchair ready to leave.

"It was my pleasure to meet you Hank. Thank you for telling me a little about your life."

Not enough, she thought. "And I'll try to treat people the way you have."

It was all she could think to say. She hoped it was enough. The aide politely said she and Hank needed to leave, and she pushed him out the door. That was it. He was gone.

Reese sat down on his bed in his unclaimed room, stunned at her feelings. She had met Hank less than 30 minutes ago, and yet she knew that she would never forget him. She had never seen such gentle strength. Reese stayed for what seemed a long time, reflecting on all they had said to one another.

Before getting up to leave, she opened the volunteer file and wondered how to report to Kelly on a visit that was so profound. She put her pen on the page and began, *Met Hank Thompson. Visited for 20 minutes. Worried about his wife. Does not want to continue blood transfusions. Wonderful man.*

Then Reese opened her iPad and wrote, "*Try to treat everyone as if they're from Hollywood." –Hank Thompson*

That night at dinner, Reese told Evan all about her visit with Hank. Every word. He listened and smiled, knowing her return had made an impact on her.

"Evan, why do you think Hank didn't want to talk about the championship? I would think that would be something he was proud of. After all, he brought it up."

Evan shrugged and spoke through another mouthful of mashed potatoes. "Because they probably lost, Reese. Guys don't like to talk about losing."

A slow smile of understanding gradually lifted her cheeks. *Of course. Why hadn't I thought of that?*

"Well he won at everything else," she said with satisfaction and got up to put her plate in the sink.

CHAPTER FOURTEEN

Mavis

In Reese's opinion, it was a story straight out of a history book. It was as if she had stepped into a live documentary and was keeping company with one of the main characters. Each time she visited Mavis, she secretly hoped to learn more details of the remarkable story. But there never seemed to be the right time to dig deeper without it having the distaste of an interview.

On this particular day, Reese found Mavis in a reflective mood. Upon walking into her room, Mavis was looking at old photographs that Reese didn't even know she had. They were spread out on her lap, with a large manila envelope underneath, serving as a tabletop. Mavis didn't even greet Reese with her usual "Well, looky here!" Instead, she simply selected a particular photo and held it out for Reese to take. It was a faded black and white photo of a young couple with serious expressions, holding suitcases.

"How much have I told you about my parents?"

"Not much, really."

"Well, that's them, Roy and Lois Dawson. They got married at seventeen. That picture is the day they left town to start a new life."

"They got married at seventeen? Was that legal?"

"Yes it was. They were in love and full of dreams. Wanted to go further south and work the cotton fields. My daddy thought they could make a livin' and find a place of their own. My grandfather said they better stick close to home where family could help 'em. But you know how that goes. Too eager to be out on their own."

Reese took another look at the couple in the photo. The girl was pretty with shoulder length hair and a well-pressed white shirtdress. He was taller than she and had his shirt buttoned all the way up. One of his arms was around her waist and the other held the larger of the two suitcases. *Shouldn't two seventeen-year-old newlyweds be smiling?*

"So off they went to southern Arkansas. And wouldn't you know it? The price of cotton fell hard. There was a horrible drought that just wiped out most plantations. Like most folks, they lost their jobs. She was pregnant with me, too."

"Did they move back home?"

Mavis smiled. "Oh no. No they didn't. 'Bout that time, the government was funding new roads in Little Rock. So you know, that seemed like the place to get a good job. And he got one, building roads. Guess they got a nice place to live, too."

"So then, you were born in Little Rock?"

Mavis' expression turned a bit somber and she nodded. "In 1934 just after New Year's."

Reese smiled and handed the photo back to Mavis. "I'd love to see a baby picture of you. Do you have one there?"

Mavis looked down at the array of photos in her lap. She nervously tapped them with her fingertips. The pause in her story hung in the air. Finally, she continued. "Even though my father had a job, there weren't many folks who could afford to have a baby in a hospital, so I was born at home."

She kept her head down and began to tap each photo again, as if doing so helped her gather her words. "You know, midwives did their best. Everybody used 'em. But my Mama, well...she had an awful time. Just awful." Tap, tap, tap. "Fever, you know. She got an infection she just couldn't fight."

Mavis never knew her mother? What do I say?

"Oh Mavis, that's sad."

"My daddy couldn't take care of no newborn child by himself and keep his job, too. And he needed that job. So he brought me back to my mama's parents. I was about seven years old when my granddaddy told me how it happened. He said, 'Your mama died givin' you birth. Couldn't be helped. And your daddy, well, his heart was broke. He didn't know much about babies and wanted to keep you in the worst way. But after months of tryin' to make it work, he got to thinkin' that maybe you'd have a better life with your grandmother and me.

So one summer day when you were about six months old, he came for a visit, holdin' you tight in his arms. Never saw a man cry as hard as your daddy cried that day. He was as broken a man as I've ever seen. I still respect him for doin' right by you.'"

Reese could picture the tall Roy Dawson with the buttoned up white shirt, cradling baby Mavis in his arms. She imagined Mavis' grandfather opening the front door to find his son-in-law standing there, tears streaming down his face, tightly holding his baby for the last time. *Did her grandfather know Roy's intention the minute he saw him?*

Mavis' voice grew stronger as she talked about her grandparents. "Granddaddy was a Baptist preacher in a little town a long ways from Little Rock. I was the only grandchild they had. They were heartbroken when my mama died and hadn't even met me until that day my daddy stood on their porch with me in his arms."

"'Gettin' the chance to raise you was more than a blessing,' my grandfather used to say. 'We lost your mama and then your daddy, but we have you, and we thank God for that.'"

"Every night my grandparents would tuck me in bed, and my grandmother would say 'Mavis, when you open your eyes tomorrow mornin', remember that you are loved with an everlastin' love.' Well, I didn't know what everlastin' meant, but I knew it had to be good just by the way she said it."

"Your grandparents sound like wonderful people, Mavis."

"Oh, they were. My granddaddy's reputation was spotless. All the folks in town, no matter their age or race, greeted him with a nod and a 'Good day, Preacher.' I loved going into town with him. Folks would tell him their problems all the time. He'd listen and then give them advice. Good advice. Then he'd quote scripture and tell them to think about it." Mavis chuckled. "You should've seen folks' faces when he did that."

"And my grandmother? I tell you what. She was always teaching me things. She taught me how to peel potatoes, make piecrust, sweep floors, fold laundry, and walk a full acre with a glass of lemonade in my hand and not spill a drop. See, Granddaddy split wood at the back of our property, and it was my job to take him lemonade. I walked that acre slow, never taking my eyes off the rim of the glass. He did so much for me; I just didn't want to spill it. When I handed it to him, he'd say, 'Mavis, I do believe there's no lemonade tastier than the one you bring me.'"

Reese enjoyed the proud look on Mavis' face and the sound of security in her voice. She used to feel that way too, when she was with Grandpa and Nadine. Reese instantly remembered sitting between them on a red cushioned pew of their little church with no air conditioning.

"Did you attend church when your grandfather preached?"

"Mmm, yes, I sure did. I got a new church dress every year, too. My grandmother would take me to town to pick out fabric. When she was done sewin', she'd call me into the parlor and show it to me. Sometimes, she added a lace collar or embroidered flowers on the hem just to surprise me. I'd walk into that church so proud. I was the preacher's pride and joy, oh yes I was.

And when the offering plate came around, my grandmother would open her little square purse with the bamboo handle and pull out the money that was just waitin' in an envelope. One day, I asked my grandmother, 'Don't the money just come back to you and Granddaddy?' She laughed and said, 'Oh Mavis, can't you see these pews need some fixin'?'"

Reese wanted to tell stories the way Mavis did. She got lost in the vision of Mavis and her grandmother sitting on pews with splitting wood. She imagined the little square purse with the bamboo handle. Did her grandmother wear white gloves? Were her hands dark and wrinkled like Mavis' are now? She wanted to ask. But Mavis had settled into her story now, and Reese could tell that questions would only interrupt the flow.

"On Sunday nights our home was full of people, mostly from church. We'd put out extra chairs along the walls of the parlor and dining room. My grandmother cooked all afternoon, hummin' and tellin' me recipe secrets as she went.

'Never forget Mavis, you got to add salt to the water first and keep stirrin' the grits. They're creamier that way.'

She made chicken, grits, collards, sweet potato pie, and cornbread muffins. As folks arrived, my grandmother would call out to them from the kitchen, 'Y'all come in now and fix a plate.'

So they'd fix a plate you know, and then sit in the parlor

and visit. My grandfather would ask each and every person how they were doin'. Later on he'd tell funny stories and get everyone laughin'. One time, I overheard these two ladies talkin' about my parents. They were busybodies you know and thought I couldn't hear them."

"I still say he died of a broken heart. Lois was everything to him."

"No, no, it was his drinkin' that killed him. After she died, whiskey was his mistress."

"Well, sure is none of our business, but thank heaven for Reverend and his wife. What would've happened to Mavis without them?"

"Poor child, she never did see what a beauty her mama was."

Mavis scowled. "That made me mad. It's hard to miss parents that you never knew. But you still don't want others tellin' tales about 'em. I wish my grandparents had told me more about them, but it just seemed disrespectful to ask too many questions. Back then, folks didn't talk about their problems."

She looked back down in her lap at the worn photos. "Everything about where I come from is right here." She carefully pulled the corner of one particular photo out from under the others. She held it up for Reese. "This is my hometown general store, where we got all our supplies."

Reese took the photo with the cracked back from Mavis. A little girl, about eight years old, stood on worn wooden steps in front of a store with curtains in the windows. In the background was a man in his fifties, a white apron covering his vest and tie.

"That little cutie pie is me," Mavis said. "And that man in the background is Mr. Foster. He owned the general store. I got the biggest story 'bout him."

Reese took another look at the man on the store porch. He was stout with a big mustache and angry face. "I'd love to hear it."

Mavis shook her head as if she still couldn't believe the story she was about to tell.

"Well, you know, it was typical for townspeople to show up at our house, askin' my grandfather for help of some kind. Usually it was money they needed. But sometimes, it was advice. Folks would sit on our porch swing and pour their hearts out to my grandfather, askin' him what they should do.

Well, I will never forget the day Beau Dobson came over. He was a handsome devil, but without the brains to match. He was so upset and out of breath, too. I wanted to know what business he had with my grandfather, so I went to my usual hidin' spot to listen. There was this big fern on a plant stand just inside our front screen door. If I crouched behind it, I could hear everything."

'Reverend, please. You gotta help me. Foster's gonna kill me, and I don't know what to do.'

"You see, Beau Dobson had helped himself to Loretta, Mr. Foster's wife. Mr. Foster came home from a business trip and found them in bed in each other's arms. He ran to get his gun and Beau ran for his life. Mr. Foster yelled out after him, 'I'm comin' for you!' Beau ran two and a half miles, all the way to our doorstep.

Let me tell you, Granddaddy was not pleased. He said that if it weren't for his very life bein' in danger, Beau Dobson should pay the piper. But my grandfather knew that Mr. Foster was a well-known white man who would bring a lynch mob for sure."

"So, you gonna tell me what to do?" Beau said.

"He was wringin' his hands and pacing on our porch. My granddaddy knew Beau had done wrong, but didn't want to see him in the hands of a lynch mob. So he hatched a plan. In just a couple of hours, he asked all his friends who owned shotguns to help. He told them to come over just before nightfall and hide in the bushes along the side of our property. Then, if Mr. Foster came with a lynch mob, my grandfather would give his men a sign to shoot their guns into the air. The mob wouldn't know where the shots were comin' from and that would send them runnin.' He told Beau to hide in the storm cellar, and when he heard those shots, to open the cellar door and run towards the back of our property until he reached the train tracks. Then he said, 'You jump the first train that comes by and ride it all the way 'til you're long gone.'

Beau said that he didn't know how to thank my grandfather. He replied, 'You can thank me by never helpin' yourself to someone else's wife again.'"

Mavis laughed, her hand over her mouth, still entertained by the memory of it all. When her laughter died down, she asked Reese, "Would you help me get these back in the envelope?"

"Wait Mavis. Aren't you going to tell me what happened to Beau? Did you see it? Were you scared?"

Mavis paused her effort to put away the photos. She smiled and looked out the window, as if to remember where she had been at the time. "Oh. Well, I was with my grandmother in the upstairs bedroom. She sat in her corner rocking chair, and I sat on the floor beside her. The light was off, and it was gettin' pretty dark in that room. I said somethin' to her, I don't remember what, and she just shushed me. Told me to stay real quiet. That's when I heard the dogs. The barkin' was far away at first, and kept gettin' louder the closer they got.

I wanted so bad to watch from the window. I knew if I went over to it, she would tell me to get back by her. I don't know what came over me, but I told her that I *was* going to watch from the window and that I'd be careful. To this day I don't know why she let me do it, but she did. Maybe she knew I was good at hidin'.

Anyway, when I got my first look, there were six men all on horses. And two dogs. They rode up fast with such a racket and stopped in front of our house. Mr. Foster got off his horse and came up to our porch, holdin' a coiled rope in his hand. My granddaddy was standin' next to the porch light, probably so all the men in the bushes could see him give the sign.

Mr. Foster yelled, "Preacher, I know you've got that nigger

hiding somewhere on your property! Now turn him over!"

My grandfather said, "What I do on my property is none of your business. I suggest you and your men go on back home."

Mr. Foster said, "Preacher, I'm not leaving until I got Dobson at the end of this rope!"

So my grandfather gave the sign to shoot. Those shots were so loud, made my heart pound right outta my chest. The horses were spooked, and the men on them started yellin' to each other. Then there were three more shots, and I was sure Mr. Dobson was gettin' the rope tied around his neck.

But then Mr. Foster yelled, "We're not done with this, Preacher!" and the horses sounded like they were runnin' away. The dogs' barks got faint, and then all was still. My grandmother and I stayed put, knowin' my grandfather would come get us. After what seemed a long time, he did.

First he hugged my grandmother. Then he told me to come sit down on the bed with him. He said, 'It's all over now. That won't happen again, Mavis. You're safe. We're all safe. And Beau Dobson should be on a train 'bout now. It's gonna be alright.'"

Reese was stunned. "I didn't realize that lynch mobs still happened in the 1940's."

"Well, let's put it this way. If a black man committed a crime down south, that's usually how the white man took care of it back then."

Reese looked back down at Mr. Foster in Mavis' old photo.

She had no words, but just shook her head in sheltered disbelief.

Mavis could see how troubled Reese looked. "That's just the way it was. Don't matter what year it is, there'll always be folks who treat other folks wrong. Always. We just gotta make sure we're not one of 'em."

Reese managed a half-hearted smile and lovingly looked at Mavis. She was sure that each wrinkle on Mavis' face was etched by life-changing events, leaving wisdom in the crevices.

It was almost lunchtime, and Mavis wanted to get to her table before the other residents. So Reese offered to push her down to the cafeteria. After saying goodbye, Reese retreated to the sunny atrium and found a familiar chair near the bird sanctuary. She needed to let this visit soak in before moving on with the rest of her day.

Once she was comfortable, Reese opened the volunteer file. She sighed at the same three boring questions staring back at her from the familiar form.

How would you describe your visit with this resident today?
Do you have any questions/concerns about this resident?
How can we help foster your relationship with this resident?
I'm not answering these today. They don't even come close.

Instead, her iPad seemed much more inviting. She turned it on and closed her eyes. Reese did her best to envision Mavis' face—her gentle brown eyes, grey hair in tight cornrows, and thin lips that lifted big wrinkled cheeks when she smiled. Eighty plus years never looked so dignified. Scenes from Mavis' remarkable story played over again in her mind. And yet, it was her closing words that moved Reese the most.

I know a woman who lived in the time of lynch mobs and hangings. A woman who has experienced discrimination during a time I've only read about in history books. And yet, she recounts those times without vengeful words or even a trace of bitterness. She doesn't advertise her experiences, but shares them sparingly with those she trusts. She doesn't advocate social causes or movements. Instead, she reasons that there will always be people who treat others wrongly. We just can't be one of them. Her attitude amazes me. And yet, maybe that attitude is exactly what has healed her scars.

CHAPTER FIFTEEN

Dorothy

"Will you come back?" She asked with sad, weak eyes.

Her frail hands were cupped around a faded blue handkerchief, her nails brittle with only a trace of pink polish from a manicure she must have done at home. Her skin was so thin that Reese could see every vein, every discolored spot that lie beneath the surface.

She had just met Dorothy for the first time today, a new resident with a bare room and nothing on the walls. Was a dresser still to come? Would her family show up with pictures or decorations?

"Oh, I'm sure to be back, Dorothy. I usually visit every week or two."

Dorothy looked at the floor around her chair and then the entire room, as if to spot something she recognized. "I'm sorry I don't have anything to offer you."

Reese was all too familiar with the apologetic look on Dorothy's face. It was one she had seen many times before when residents realized that their belongings, their food supply, and even their power to offer a guest a glass of lemonade is extinct. It was one of the most heart-wrenching moments of any visit.

"It's ok, Dorothy. I've just enjoyed getting to know you a little." Reese always tried to sound upbeat, as if it was completely normal to have a conversation for the first time while sitting with a stranger on his or her bed.

"I won't be here long, you know. Once things get straightened out, I'll be going back home. I've gotta pick the tomatoes. They're probably ripe by now."

"So you have a garden at home?"

Dorothy nodded. "A big one. Radishes, squash, cucumbers, everything."

"Wow, that sounds wonderful. You must really know a lot about gardening. Maybe you could give me a few tips?" Reese liked to affirm and show interest in their lives at home, yet she had to be careful not to stir up feelings of resentment about being in the nursing home.

"Well, I don't know about that. You just have to plant at the right times and you know, keep an eye on things. What day is it? I know those tomatoes are ready."

"It's Thursday, Dorothy. Do you have family or a neighbor that can check on your garden?"

This too, was usually a sketchy subject. Each situation was so different, and a resident's understanding of reality so hard to evaluate in the beginning. Reese never knew where questions about family would lead, or if the answers would even be accurate.

"I have a son who checks on me. He doesn't live too far away."

"That's good. Maybe he can check on the tomatoes."

Dorothy nodded with a distant look in her eyes. Reese waited, but the tiny figure in her worn, floral dress offered no more information. Reese figured her son hadn't had time to bring by her personal items, or he lived much farther away than Dorothy thought. Or, there was no son at all. That was a possibility, too.

Reese usually kept first visits short, and for the most part, this one with Dorothy was quite uneventful. She hadn't been able to connect with her or learn much of her background. Dorothy had appeared dazed, and focused solely on her tomatoes. And on this particular chilly day, with grey clouds and mist in the air, Reese didn't have the desire to keep trying.

"It was a pleasure to meet you, Dorothy. Don't worry, they will take good care of you." *There. I can go now.*

Reese left Dorothy's room with a bored, empty feeling. She had been visiting Oak Hills for almost twelve months beyond the end of the Adopt a Neighbor program. After all this time, she felt protective of the residents and grateful for all she had learned from them. But for reasons she couldn't explain, she was becoming tired of it all.

I wish I could get together with them somewhere else. Like a coffee shop. And they drove on their own. Or better yet, came to my apartment.

After only one visit today, Reese just wanted to be home on

her comfortable couch with the soft, green blanket. She wanted to put on her favorite music and let Max curl up on her feet. Reese headed toward the atrium and signed out with no hesitation.

This is no big deal. I'll come back in a week or two. I just need a break.

That night, Reese waited until Evan was watching the news and then went into their bedroom to call Monica.

"It might be time to find a new gig," Monica advised. Reese knew she could count on her best friend to offer an honest assessment once again.

"Monica, you know how much soul searching I did to come to peace with these visits. Once I felt like Nadine would be happy about it, the residents became even more important to me. Besides, I have some regulars, and I'm probably the only one who visits them. I'd hate to leave them with no one."

"Okay, but Reese, this isn't your *job*. It's not like we're talking about salary, or hours, or benefits. Look, you're the only one who can decide what this is worth. And it sounds to me like you're tired of it. Why don't you just take a break and see if you miss it?"

As she lay on their bed tracing the circular pattern on their comforter with her finger, her friend's words soaked in. *You're the only one who can decide what this is worth.*

"But if I take a break, I'm afraid I won't go back."

"Pretty telling, don't you think?" Monica responded. "Look, this obviously isn't about them. It's about you, letting go. More than a year ago, you didn't want to commit and now you can't let go. You've already proven yourself faithful. So what's wrong with just pulling the plug?"

"They're people, Monica. Incredible people. And I see them differently now. Are they from another time? Yes, but that's what's so amazing about it. They've lived through a lot of stuff yet have these resilient attitudes. Their circumstances are different, but they have the same feelings and concerns we do. And I've gained a lot by just listening to their stories."

"That's cool. It really is. But don't you have to just move on at some point? You said yourself that you're getting tired of it. I mean, it's great that you learned to appreciate old people, but that time might be over."

Reese was silent. She had called Monica for the very purpose of constructive feedback. But she never thought that Monica wouldn't understand. Never thought that she wouldn't see the value of elderly people, the way Reese did now. "You know, Monica, it took me awhile. But I've learned that it's not just about their cool stories. It's about them wanting to connect, wanting to share their wisdom before it's buried. They have a lot to offer. They really *do*."

Monica breathed a gentle sigh. "Ree, I didn't mean to hurt your feelings or insult them. And maybe I don't get it. But as your friend, I can tell you need a break. Maybe you should just take a leave of absence, and then go back in a few months or so."

"Yeah, maybe. I do tend to take an all or nothing approach sometimes."

"Ya think?" Reese could hear the smile in Monica's voice. She was glad they ended their conversation on a good note. But she had wanted the call to Monica to answer her question, to give her that confident reason for sticking with it or letting it go for good. But neither rose to the surface.

Reese got comfortable on her stomach, clutching a pillow at just the right spot to rest her chin. *If Nadine were still here, she'd know what I should do.* She closed her eyes and tried to imagine sitting back at Nadine and Grandpa's kitchen table. Perhaps they would be eating strawberries out of that chipped green mixing bowl. Reese could clearly recall Nadine's weathered, but still lovely face. She could see the tiny, silver hoop earrings that Nadine wore every day and her shoulder length, gray hair pulled behind her ears.

Often when Reese wanted to talk, Nadine would gently pat Grandpa's forearm and say, "My handsome Ray, I think this might be girl time."

He'd smile and excuse himself. "That's fine. I've got a workbench calling my name."

Reese longed to tell Nadine how she felt. She spoke her thoughts out loud, her words absorbed by the pillow. "After my work obligation ended, I didn't want to keep visiting them. I thought it would mean betraying you."

Nadine's hand reached for Reese's. "Honey, what ever made you think that?"

"Because I couldn't forgive myself for not visiting you more often after we had to put you in the nursing home. I let too many things get in the way. And then you died and my chances were gone." Reese kept her eyes squeezed tight, and held her breath, hoping to visualize Nadine's response.

Nadine was no longer at the table with her. Instead, she was drying the dishes, happily singing her favorite hymn, the one Reese heard countless times over the years: "Great is Thy faithfulness, oh God my Father, morning by morning new mercies I see…all I have needed Thy hand hath provided, great is Thy faithfulness Lord unto me."

*Morning by morning new mercies I see…*Nadine sang those words with such confidence, the type of confidence for which Reese admired her.

How many times had Reese needed a boost of confidence, and Nadine gently fed it to her, like corn in a child's hand stretched through the fence for a goat? She remembered pouring her heart out to Nadine about a school friend who was moving out of state. Reese was in 8th grade at the time and felt abandoned. "She can't leave! We're best friends!"

Nadine had put her arm around Reese. "Yes, she can. She loved you and you loved her while she lived here. That's what matters."

So was that Nadine's secret to life? Was it as simple as loving those around you in the moment?

Reese turned flat on her back, releasing the pillow she had so tightly clutched. She stretched her arms wide open across the bed and took in long, deep breaths. For reasons she could not explain, a feeling of gentle peace gradually filled her, as if she had breathed it in like oxygen.

She smiled and slowly sat up on the bed, her guilt and worry beginning to subside. She heard muffled voices from the living room and walked out to find Evan watching a nighttime comedy show, looking comfortable and close to sleep.

"Babe, why don't we go to bed."

"Yup," he agreed, rubbing his eyes and slowly sitting up. "Did you come to a decision?" he asked through a yawn.

Reese smiled and shrugged, "Not really, but I've got a feeling the morning will let me know."

FROM THE AUTHOR

A few years ago, I found myself transformed by incredible bits of wisdom gifted me by the residents of a local nursing home. To be honest, I hadn't expected their stories to be so relatable. After all, they were members of a very different generation than mine. Yet their stories strengthened my resolve and softened the hard lines of some of my attitudes. I hated to think their words would fade away and never find a home in anyone else's heart.

According to Merriam-Webster, the definition of elderly is: *rather old, especially being past middle age.* I'd like to suggest a different definition. *Elderly—one who's been there, done that, learned from it, and can give timeless truth.* By that definition, we can all claim to be elderly works in progress.

I hope you'll join the community where life lessons are shared and words of gold are spoken across generations. You're always welcome at ***http://www.wordsofgold.me***

ACKNOWLEDGEMENTS

Jeff, no one speaks words of gold into my life the way you do. The road of life has been rugged at times, harvesting growth in both of us. This season of our marriage is by far the sweetest and I am so grateful for your constant encouragement and pep talks. You truly are my knight.

Grant and Mitch, there are no finer sons on earth. Your integrity, brave hearts, and pursuit of God continue to wow me. I know you will speak words of gold into your families that promote love and respect. In case you didn't know, you are our heroes.

Jenna and Ashley, you are proof that praying for whom our sons would marry paid off big time. I have so much love and admiration for you both. You are living examples of genuine beauty, honesty, and devotion. The fabric of our family is stronger and more beautiful because of you.

Brigham, Marshall, and Judah, you have taken my joy to a new level. Loving grandchildren must be experienced to be truly understood. Well, I understand now. I will do my best to speak words of gold into your lives. I hope one day, you will understand just how much your young lives teach the rest of us.

And Ashley, thank you for agreeing to be my editor. You offered the perfect dose of suggestion, correction, and much needed inspiration. Your love of story is contagious and your knowledge provided me a framework in which to learn. Every writer should be so lucky.

CHAPTER NOTES

Chapter One - Caprice
Many employers support and encourage volunteering. If you'd like to learn more about volunteer opportunities in your community, consider this site:
http://www.volunteermatch.org/

Chapter Two - Lydia
If you'd like to learn more about Multiple Sclerosis or learn how you can make a difference for those suffering from this disease, visit:
National Multiple Sclerosis Society
http://www.nationalmssociety.org/about-multiple-sclerosis/index.aspx

Chapter Three - Florence
Alzheimer's currently affects more than five million people in America. Approximately two thirds are women. To learn more, visit:
http://www.alzorg/alzheimers_disease_what_is_alzheimers.asp
National Institute on Aging
http://www.nia.nih.gov/alzheimers

Chapter Four - Eleanor
There are multiple support groups for those who have lost their loved ones while serving in the military.

This website offers support to survivors of veterans:
http://www.taps.org/survivors
If you'd like to show your support to our military or their families, visit:
http://bluestarfam.org

Chapter Five - Dennis
For more information on respiratory disease, visit:
http://www.emphysemafoundation.org/

Chapter Six - Jeanie
Crime, natural disasters, and other crises affect every community. To learn how you can help to "keep good going" in your community, visit:
National Organization for Victim Assistance
http://www.trynova.org/
The Salvation Army
http://www.salvationarmyusa.org/usn/

Chapter Seven - Rose
Mentoring moments have the power to change lives. To find out more about mentoring opportunities in your area, call your local Social Services agency or visit the following:
National Mentoring Partnership
http://www.mentoring.org/
Big Brothers Big Sisters
www.bbbs.org

Chapter Eight - Monica

Most people wish they had more time to nurture friendships. The following sites offer ideas:

http://friendship.about.com/od/Improving_Friendships/
http://girlfriendcircles.com/

Chapter Nine - Nadine and Grandpa

For more information about the power of intergenerational relationships, visit:

Generations United
http://www.gu.org/
Intergenerational Activities Sourcebook
http://pubs.cas.psu.edu/freepubs/pdfs/agrs91.pdf

Chapter Ten - Earl

All must navigate the road to forgiving someone or being forgiven. Quite often, getting help from friends or professionals is an important step.

Visit this site and search forgiveness:
http://www.focusonthefamily.com
Counseling resources:
http://newlife.com

Chapter Eleven - Skip

The reasons that people fall into addictive behaviors are vast but the damaging results of these behaviors are all too common. To understand more about addiction, consider:

American Society of Addiction Medicine
http://www.asam.org/for-the-public/definition-of-addiction
Psychologytoday.com
http://www.psychologytoday.com/basics/addiction

Chapter Twelve - Evan
Each grief journey is unique and cannot be compared to the grief of others. If you or someone you know is grieving, help is available from a multitude of resources.
To find grief support groups near you:
www.griefshare.org

Chapter Thirteen - Hank
Hospice does compassionate work for the terminally ill. For more information about their services, please visit their website.
Hospice Foundation
http://hospicefoundation.org

Chapter Fourteen - Mavis
Listening to the stories of older generations is a valuable way to learn more about life.
http://petenali.hubpages.com/hub/ten-reasons-why-you-need-to-talk-with-an-elderly-person
https://www.growingbolder.com/

Chapter Fifteen - Dorothy
Each day holds the potential to make even a small difference in someone's life. Here are two sites with ideas:
http://www.virtuesforlife.com/100-ways-to-be-kinder/
http://www.kindspring.org/ideas/

The websites noted above relate directly to each chapter and are meant to be a starting point for further information. There are a myriad of other possible resources and the author does not claim to be familiar with every aspect of the listed websites nor does she claim to endorse them. Self-guided research is assumed.

For more about this book and posts from the author, visit the website and blog ***http://www.wordsofgold.me***

62454242R00098

Made in the USA
Lexington, KY
07 April 2017